Tutti's
Promise

"[A] gripping tale. . . . The spirited, realistic dialogue brings the characters to life. . . . That the family survived to have this powerful, heartening tale told cannot fail to move readers."
— *Booklist*

"*Tutti's Promise* is an engrossing story of hope, family, survival, and identity."
— *Stephen D. Smith, PhD,*
Executive Director of the USC Shoah Foundation

"Fishman tells the tale of her mother's family with elegance and a great sense of suspense."
— *Kirkus Reviews*

"History comes alive in Fishman's capable hands as a writer telling the story of her mother and achieving the family's eternal desire to always remember."
— *Michelle Jacobs, The US Review of Books*

Nautilus Book Awards
Silver Medal
Middle Grades: Fiction

Benjamin Franklin Award
Two Silver Medals
•
Young Reader:
Fiction (8-12 years)
•
Best New Voice:
Children's/YA

A Notable Social Studies
Trade Book for Young
People

Tutti's Promise

A novel based on a family's
true story of courage and hope
during the Holocaust

K. Heidi Fishman

MB PUBLISHING

Tutti's Promise: A novel based on a family's true story of courage and hope during the Holocaust

Text copyright © 2017 K. Heidi Fishman
Design and layout © 2017 PageWave Graphics Inc., www.pagewavegraphics.com
MB Publishing, LLC, www.mbpublishing.com
First Edition
Tutti's Promise/by K. Heidi Fishman
p. cm.

Summary: Based upon actual recollections, documents, and interviews about their ordeal during the Holocaust in the Netherlands, this is the remarkable story of the Lichtenstern family—of their courage and perseverance, determination and hope—during the darkest days of human history.

ISBN, softcover: 978-0-9908430-1-6
ISBN, e-book (epub): 978-0-9908430-9-2
ISBN, e-book (mobi): 978-0-9913646-6-4

Library of Congress Control Number: 2016918422

Note to Readers:
While reading this story, you may refer to the Historical Notes section in the back of the book for further information and explanations. To learn more about this story, please visit www.kheidifishman.com. There you'll find more photographs and historical documents, Ruth "Tutti" Lichtenstern Fishman's video testimony, research links, and discussion questions.

For my mother, Ruth "Tutti" Lichtenstern Fishman.

Thank you for being an inspiration to so many and for showering your family with unconditional love.

— K. Heidi Fishman

Contents

Between 1938 and early 1940, Germany annexed Austria and Czechoslovakia and invaded Poland, Denmark, and Norway. In May 1940, Germany took over Belgium, Luxembourg, France, and the Netherlands.

The Lichtenstern Family Tree

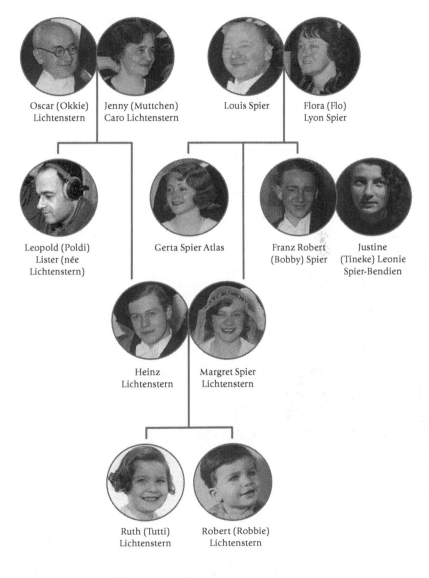

Oscar (Okkie) Lichtenstern

Jenny (Muttchen) Caro Lichtenstern

Louis Spier

Flora (Flo) Lyon Spier

Leopold (Poldi) Lister (née Lichtenstern)

Gerta Spier Atlas

Franz Robert (Bobby) Spier

Justine (Tineke) Leonie Spier-Bendien

Heinz Lichtenstern

Margret Spier Lichtenstern

Ruth (Tutti) Lichtenstern

Robert (Robbie) Lichtenstern

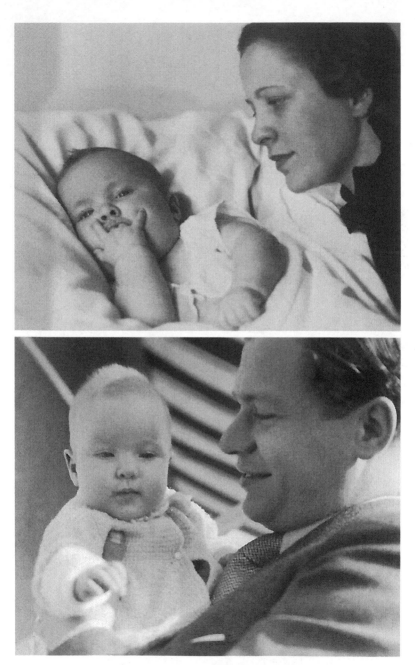

Tutti with her parents, Margret and Heinz (1935)

Prologue

Tutti, eighty years old, was sitting outside the principal's office.

She wasn't a student, of course, but was a guest at the school. The principal had invited her to talk with the eighth-graders about her childhood under the Nazis.

This was not the first school Tutti had visited to tell her story, and so by now, she knew by heart what she wanted to say. The first time she had spoken to a group of children, she had carefully written out her talk on index cards. Now she left the cards at home.

My name is Ruth Lichtenstern Fishman, but everyone calls me Tutti, she always began. I was born on July 17, 1935, in Cologne, Germany.

Two years earlier, Adolph Hitler had come to power, and the Nazis started passing anti-Jewish laws, keeping Jews out of certain jobs and schools and burning books by Jewish authors. Then in September 1935, the Nazis told us that we were no longer German citizens.

My father and grandfather worked for a metals-trading company called Oxyde. The owner was Jewish, and he decided to move his business to the Netherlands. So in 1936, my family moved there, too. But four years later, we found out that we hadn't moved far enough away from danger . . .

Tutti Lichtenstern Fishman, age 80

1

Invasion

May 10, 1940

❦

Tutti awoke with a start. Robbie was crying. She heard strange sounds outside—big booms. Juffie, the nanny, was rocking two-year-old Robbie and trying to get him back to sleep. Tutti, nearly five years old, climbed out of bed and found Mammi and Pappi peering out the window in their pajamas.

"Mammi, what is that noise?" asked Tutti.

"Margret, look who's here," Heinz said. "Did all that commotion outside wake you, Tutti?"

"Yes, Pappi," she answered, rubbing her eyes.

Mammi quickly picked her up. "Whatever it is, it's far away," she said. "Don't be scared."

Mammi brought Tutti back to the nursery and tucked her into bed. She collected Robbie from Juffie and patted his back until he settled down. Then she gently laid him in his bed and pulled the soft blanket up to his shoulders. She kissed Tutti on the forehead, smoothed her red curls, and picked her doll up off the floor, placing it next to her. "*Gute Nacht,*" she whispered. "Juffie will stay right here, so there's no need to be frightened. I'll let you know what all of this is about in the morning."

❧   ❧   ❧

But when the sun came up, with the buzz of airplane motors in the distance, Tutti became focused on something new. She wondered why the radio was on so early and why Pappi scowled and gripped the sides of his armchair as he listened to it. "Mammi, why is the radio on? What is Pappi listening to?"

"Shh, Tutti," said Mammi. "Pappi needs to hear the news."

"*German troops have crossed the Dutch frontier and are in contact with our border forces. There have been landing attempts by enemy aircraft and paratroopers,*" squawked the radio.

"Pappi, why is the radio so loud?" Tutti asked.

"Shh, Tutti," Pappi insisted.

"Heinz, please turn down the radio," said Mammi, lifting her eyebrows slightly. "The children are awake now," she said, scooting them into the kitchen for breakfast.

"*The bridges over the Meuse and IJssel have been destroyed.*"

Robbie began to cry. Mammi picked him up and walked to the window.

"*At least seventy German planes were shot down, with Germans using Dutch prisoners as cover.*"

Tutti ran back to the living room. "Pappi, can we turn on some music? Robbie doesn't like this man's voice and neither do I."

"*Um Gottes Willen!*" Pappi bellowed. "Margret, please keep the children with you. This news is important." He got up to adjust the dial and remained standing beside the radio, scowling.

Mammi took Tutti by the hand and led her away, but it was impossible not to hear what the announcer was saying.

"Paratroopers have landed at strategic points near Rotterdam, The Hague, Amsterdam, and other large cities . . ."

All three sat at the table, but Mammi stood up a minute later. "Tutti, please help Robbie with his breakfast. Juffie's not here. She left to make sure her sister is all right. I'll be right back." Mammi went into the living room and turned down the blaring radio, but she didn't return to the table right away.

"And now I will read Queen Wilhelmina's speech to the people of the Netherlands," Tutti heard the announcer say. She listened carefully, but he said a lot of words she didn't understand:

"To my people! After our country has scrupulously maintained neutrality, last night the German troops suddenly attacked our territory without the slightest warning . . . . I herewith protest against this unprecedented violation of good faith and condemn

Tutti and Robbie Lichtenstern (1940)

the attack as a flagrant violation of international law and decency. My government and I will now do our duty. You must do yours with the utmost watchfulness and with inner calmness and devotion . . ."

Heinz turned off the radio and stood to give Margret a hug. "The phones aren't working. We have to check on our parents," he said.

"You're right. They must be worried about us, too."

"I'll go to my parents' apartment first and then Flo and Louis'. It won't take me long. I'll be back in an hour or two," Heinz said, squeezing his wife's hand.

When Mammi came back into the kitchen, Tutti saw she had tears in her eyes. She hadn't really understood what the announcer was saying, but she knew it wasn't good news.

❧

gute Nacht (goo•tuh nah<u>kht</u>): good night (German)

Juffie (yoof•ee; oo, as in the oo in took): A nickname meaning "Missy" (Dutch)

Tutti (too•tee; oo, as in the oo in took): Ruth Lichtenstern's nickname

um Gottes Willen (oom gawt•ehs vill•uhn): for God's sake (German)

2

A Date with Uncle Bobby

Summer 1940

❧

Within five days of the invasion, the Dutch army surrendered, and the Germans marched into Amsterdam. A small fraction of the population joined the Dutch Nazi Party (NSB), but hundreds of thousands of Netherlanders rebelled through acts of brave resistance—going on strike, creating underground newspapers, and hiding Jews. Some engaged in sabotage, such as cutting phone lines, destroying rail lines, and disabling German vehicles.

Those Jews who tried to flee were mostly unsuccessful. The country's geography and the dangerous Nazi-infested North Sea made escape essentially impossible.

If only the land had had a different topography. If only it had not been devoid of mountains and forests, which would have provided sanctuary and cover. If only the surrounding countries had not already fallen under German control. Then the fate of the Jews in the Netherlands might have been much different than it was.

But Tutti was blissfully unaware of all this . . . and was especially happy one summer day after she turned five . . .

❧   ❧   ❧

"Come, Tutti. Let's get you dressed. Your uncle Bobby will be here soon." Mammi opened the closet and easily slid the hangers across the rod one by one until she found the dress she was looking for. "How about this one?" She pulled out a blue dress with white trim. Tutti had worn it only a couple of times and just loved the way it swished around her legs when she twirled.

"Mammi, where is Uncle Bobby taking me to lunch?" Tutti was already shedding her play clothes.

"The Blauwe Theehuis in the Vondelpark. Do you think you'll like that?"

"Oh, the Vondelpark!" Tutti jumped up and down. "Can we feed the ducks?"

"I'm sure you can." Margret smiled at the child's enthusiasm and felt her heart fill with love. For Tutti, little had changed since Germany's invasion. But for Margret, there was tremendous concern: How would each new policy affect them? The Nazis had recently ordered Jewish-owned businesses to hang up signs that read "Jewish business." How would Heinz's job be affected? And how would she keep her family safe?

Margret held the dress for Tutti to step into and then buttoned up the back. She watched as Tutti spun around and her little dress flared out. How simple things could bring her child such joy! Margret would do whatever it took to make sure that Tutti could enjoy these little pleasures—a new dress and lunch with her handsome young uncle—and not have to worry about the war. She helped Tutti with her socks and shoes and completed the outfit with her new coat. Just as they were buttoning it, there was a knock at the door.

Tutti about to leave on her date with Margret's brother, Tutti's Uncle Bobby

"Uncle Bobby!" Tutti ran to Bobby and threw her body into his open arms. Bobby, dressed in a blue suit and striped tie, his hair smartly parted to the side, lifted a package above his head so Tutti's embrace wouldn't crush it. He laughed at her exuberance and returned the hug.

"Is that present for me?" Tutti asked.

"No, sweetheart, this gift is for Robbie. It's a pony."

"Oh, he'll like that. But why can't I have a present too, Uncle Bobby?" she protested.

"I'm taking you out to lunch. I brought this for your brother since he's too little to join us. Now which would you rather have, a present or an afternoon out with your favorite uncle?"

Tutti thought it would be nice to have both but understood that it wasn't something to say out loud. Anyway, she soon forgot all about Robbie's present because the afternoon was so much fun. She felt like a teenager on a first date.

Her uncle ordered them pancakes with jam. Tutti tried to remember all the manners her parents had taught her. She put her napkin on her lap and didn't use her fingers to eat her pancake, except once. The hardest rule to remember—because she had so much to tell her uncle—was not to talk with her mouth full!

For dessert, Bobby ordered a whole tray of little cakes—with pink and white and yellow icing, and little candied violets and tiny silver balls. They were so beautiful she could hardly stand to eat them. "Enjoy them now, Tuttchen," her uncle said, taking a bite of one. "If this war goes on, there won't be so many nice things to eat."

When Bobby finished his coffee, they strolled to the pond. Tutti crouched by the water's edge and watched how the ducklings followed their mother around. "Are you and Aunt Tineke going to have a baby, Uncle Bobby?"

"Someday . . . that's certainly the hope. Why do you ask, Tutti?"

"Well, because then I could have a cousin to play with," she said, throwing a handful of crumbs to the ducks. "All of mine live far away. Why did everyone move to England?"

Bobby looked uncomfortable. "Oh, Tutti, people move for lots of reasons." He threw the last of the crumbs into the water and brushed off his hands, one against the other. "Maybe your mammi can explain it better than I can. But you know what? I'll see what I can do about having a baby soon—just for you."

Blauwe Theehuis (blau • uh tay • house): Blue Teahouse (Dutch)

Tuttchen (tuhtch • ehn): An endearing nickname for Tutti (German)

3

Egbert

Early October 1940

✤

Heinz was startled by the ringing phone. He looked at the clock—eleven thirty. Jumping out of bed, he grabbed his robe and hurried to the study to see who was calling.

"*Hallo?*"

"Heinz, this is Egbert. I need to talk with you."

Egbert de Jong was Heinz's friend and colleague, someone he had known for years. But a call like this, especially at this time of night, was quite unusual.

Before the German invasion, Egbert had worked for the Dutch government as the state minister in charge of nonferrous (non-iron) metals. As a metals trader, Heinz interacted with him constantly, and the two men had become true friends.

"Egbert, now? It's almost midnight."

"*Ja.* I know. Sorry, but this is important. I'd like to come and meet with you tomorrow."

"Sure, come to the office—"

"No, this isn't something to be discussed at the office. It's better if I come to your house tomorrow. Tell Margret not to fuss."

✤   ✤   ✤

The next afternoon, Margret served biscuits and coffee to Heinz and Egbert, who tapped his foot and played with his spoon, hardly touching his cup. Margret did her best to pretend not to notice and tried to make small talk, but the conversation flagged.

"Egbert, what is it? What do you need to discuss with me?" said Heinz finally.

"It's a long story and I hardly know where to begin," his friend replied. "Can we go into your study and speak alone? Margret, please excuse us. I don't want to bore you with shoptalk."

Heinz closed the door to the study and motioned for Egbert to sit down, more puzzled and more apprehensive than ever. He'd had trouble getting back to sleep after Egbert's phone call the night before, and now his head ached. "Please, Egbert, you must explain." And Egbert finally did.

The Germans had asked him to stay on as their German state minister for nonferrous metals in the Netherlands and guide the Dutch metals trade for Hitler's regime, the Third Reich. Heinz was not surprised; Egbert was highly educated—fluent in five languages—and had polished manners. He was also extraordinarily good at his job in the metals industry.

"I thought it over long and hard, and I have accepted the job," Egbert said. Somewhat uncomfortably, he added, "You understand it's not because I want to help the Germans, but I felt I had no choice. And I think—I hope—that I might someday be able to do something to stymie them."

Heinz said nothing. He was trying to make sense of what he was hearing.

"Heinz, let me bring you up to date," Egbert went on. "The Germans have appointed a Paul Zimmermann as the commissioner for the Office of Reichs Metal. This Nazi general likes me—trusts me. Heaven knows why . . . I must be a good actor. Anyway, over the course of the past few months, this General Zimmermann has become convinced that I am completely behind the Nazi cause."

"Egbert, that's ridiculous!"

"Well, of course it is, Heinz! But it's a good thing he thinks so, because now he trusts me with incredibly sensitive information—which is why I'm here. Three weeks ago, Zimmermann summoned me to Berlin for a meeting. When we met, he told me about the Nazis' plan for the Netherlands."

Heinz sat up straighter in his seat as his friend continued: "Zimmermann swore me to secrecy, but I can't keep this a secret. It's too horrendous. He said that the Germans are planning to take over all businesses that are run by Jews. First, the firms will have to register; then, Aryan directors and supervisors will be appointed. Once they are in control of the companies, they will ship the Jewish workers and owners to Poland."

"So they are going to steal our livelihoods right out from under us?" asked Heinz.

"Heinz, you aren't listening. They aren't merely going to take your job—they are going to send you to Poland! All Jews are to be deported and forced to live in ghettos or assigned to work camps or . . ." Egbert didn't finish his sentence. He simply grimaced and shook his head.

Unbelievable! Unthinkable! Heinz was out of his chair and pacing around the study now. *Forced deportations? Work camps? No, it wasn't possible.* "Egbert, there are over 140,000 Jews in this country. They can't possibly . . ."

"Heinz, that's their plan. You've heard the news. You know how bad it is already. Jews by the thousands are

Heinz Lichtenstern

being forced to live in ghettos in Poland. They are cut off from the outside world. There are reports of starvation, beatings, shootings, and epidemics in these ghettos. Italy and Japan recently signed a pact with Germany. Vichy France has devised its own laws to discriminate against Jews. No place is safe anymore. These brutes want to take over the entire world with their sick ideology. All they care about is power . . . and that means they're ruthless. All people whom these Nazi thugs consider inferior are in danger—especially the Jews. But . . . I think I can protect you."

"How?" Heinz asked. His head hurt and he was struggling to process what Egbert was saying.

"This is how I figure it. The Germans will need metal for their war. You are the leading metals trader in the country. I will tell them that you are essential."

"Egbert, I don't want to help the Germans!"

"You don't have to, at least not too much. We just need them to *think* you're assisting. I'm going to talk with Josef Sax from Hoogovens Steel, as well. Do you know him?"

Heinz nodded. "He's a good man."

"And I was thinking about Leopold Oberländer. What do you think of him?"

"Egbert, Oberländer is exceptionally smart. He knows everything about manufacturing. I think he even holds some patents."

"Good . . . then I can protect them this way, too. I've already put in an urgent request with the authorities for you to come to my office in The Hague. Since you are now acting director of Oxyde, this shouldn't seem an unreasonable request. I want the Germans to see that I consider you indispensable."

"All right, Egbert. I trust you. And I appreciate your wanting to help me. But I also want to see if I can get to England or America."

"It's too late for that, Heinz!" said Egbert.

Heinz hung his head and rubbed his eyes.

Egbert was pained at seeing his friend's distress. "Heinz, maybe I'm wrong," he said. "Perhaps there *will* be a way."

The friends clasped hands before leaving Heinz's study to rejoin Margret, who was reading to the children. Egbert bent down to give Tutti and Robbie a parting kiss on their foreheads and then embraced Margret and Heinz in turn. "Stay strong, you two," he whispered. "And stay safe. We'll get through this."

❧

hallo (hah•loh): hello (Dutch)

ja (yah): yes (Dutch)

4

Entrust

March 1941

❧

After his meeting with Egbert, Heinz had only one thing on his mind: money. Every cent mattered. He made phone calls. He talked with his closest friends. As the months passed, he counted every guilder.

Egbert's plan—for the Germans to regard Heinz as an indispensable metals expert—was well and good, but Heinz had plans of his own: Egbert was going to help him protect his family—and save his friends. He would be ready if Egbert's request for him to travel to The Hague was approved.

It was a long winter of waiting. And as he waited, he felt the Nazis tightening their noose around his neck. That fall, the Germans began requiring that businesses owned by Jews, or having one Jewish partner or director, be registered. Egbert had been right. As 1940 turned to 1941, the Germans ordered that all radios be registered. And in February, after a Dutch Nazi was killed by a Jew, over 400 Jews were rounded up and deported from Amsterdam. Heinz couldn't wait any longer—he had to put his plan into action now.

❧ ❧ ❧

"Mr. de Jong, this is Heinz Lichtenstern." He was calling Egbert from the office and was aware that anything he said might be heard by Egbert's supervisor. His friend's phone could be bugged, or Zimmermann could be sitting in the office right next to Egbert.

"Ah, Lichtenstern. Good to hear from you," replied Egbert. "How can I help?"

"I have an important matter to discuss with you," Heinz replied. "You told me to keep you informed of all possible sources for different alloys. I've identified a potential prospect, and I'm afraid that if we wait much longer, we might lose out. The deal might get taken by another buyer."

"Lichtenstern, I knew I could count on you. You have good instincts. Shall I come to Amsterdam later today?"

"Yes, as soon as you can. I need your advice on this particular opportunity."

When he hung up the phone, he sighed with relief. Egbert knew what he was talking about, but the Nazis wouldn't.

✧ ✧ ✧

While Heinz waited for Egbert to arrive, he paced the floor. He went to the window constantly and looked for his friend. What if Egbert didn't come alone? What if he brought a supervisor? Then his whole plan would fall apart.

Margret brought him a small glass of brandy, and he sat down without uttering a word. The brandy was strong and warmed his throat and chest. He needed this. He reached into his pocket for his cigarettes and then remembered he had smoked the last one on the way home from the office. His hands shook as he took another sip of the brandy.

"Margret, do we have any more cigarettes?"

She left the room and returned with half a pack. What would he ever do without her?

When at last the bell rang, Heinz saw that Egbert was not alone. With him were his wife, Jo, and his three daughters. "*Goedendag!*" said Egbert as the family came into the house and out of the early spring rain.

"Egbert, I was worried. You're an hour late."

"The trains aren't as reliable as they used to be, Heinz."

"Margret, Jo—Egbert and I need to discuss business first. We'll join you ladies for a coffee later."

While Tutti led Egbert's daughters to her room to play, Margret and Jo made their way to the kitchen. Once the two men were in the study, Heinz slid shut the heavy pocket door and handed Egbert a thick envelope. Egbert peered inside and his eyes widened. "How much is this?"

"It's 130,000 guilders. It's all the money I've been able to scrape together over the past five months."

"What do you want me to do with it?"

"I want you to take care of it for me. When we left Germany in 1936, the Nazis took nearly everything. They only allowed me to leave with a small fraction of what I owned. *They* called it a flight tax for emigrating. *I* called it highway robbery. They will come after my money again. You told me so yourself. Please take this."

"Heinz, this is a lot of money. Are you sure?"

"Egbert, I actually thought that when we moved to Amsterdam, we would be all right. Can you believe it?" Heinz gave something between a laugh and a snort and then crushed his cigarette into the ashtray. "I thought they would leave this country alone. I should have followed my brother and taken Margret and the children to England. I made a mistake." Heinz cleared his throat and looked straight into

Egbert de Jong at his office in The Hague

the eyes of his friend. "I beg you." His voice cracked, and he hesitated. He knew that what he was about to ask could put his friend in danger, but he was desperate. "Egbert, do you know Jakob Jorysch in Basel?"

"Of course. I did plenty of deals with him when I was still a trader myself. But what does he have to do with this?"

"There are ways to procure passports for South American countries. If you can contact him . . ."

"You don't have to say another word," Egbert said. "I understand. I will protect your money and use it to get you a passport if I can."

"Egbert, not only me—all of my friends at Oxyde! My parents. Margret's parents. Look. Here, I have another envelope for you. But you have to be even more cautious with this one."

Egbert took the envelope and glanced inside. It contained several small photos, each with a name and a birthdate written on the back.

Heinz continued to speak as Egbert shuffled through the photos. "All these families contributed to that pile of money I gave you. Use the money. Use it to help us get out of here. But don't let this envelope with the pictures fall into the wrong hands. It could land *you* in one of those camps we're all trying to avoid."

"You can trust me. I'll do this. And I'll return whatever is left after this war is finished and life is normal again."

"That day can't come soon enough," replied Heinz. "Let's find Jo and Margret and have a drink."

❧

guilders (**gil**•duhrs): Dutch currency (English)

goedendag (<u>**khoo**</u>•duh•dah<u>**kh**</u>): good day (Dutch)

5

Changes

Fall 1941

❧

"I'm all ready for school, Mammi," Tutti announced as she came into the kitchen. She was wearing the blouse and the skirt that she and Mammi had laid out yesterday evening, and her curly hair was neatly brushed.

Mammi gave her a hug. "Pappi, doesn't Tutti look pretty for her first day of school?" Tutti held out her skirt and did a little twirl for Pappi, but he didn't glance up from his paper and seemed not to have heard Mammi.

"Heinz, put that newspaper down and give your daughter a proper 'Good morning,' please. Now doesn't she look nice on her first day of school?"

This time Heinz looked up. "You do indeed, Tutti." He folded the paper, put it in his briefcase, and gave her a big smile. But when he turned to Margret, the smile was practically gone. "Sorry, but I have a busy day ahead of me. I'll be home late." He put on his suit coat and headed out the door.

Mammi took a deep breath and shook her head. Then she smiled at Tutti as she placed a plate with apple slices, bread, cheese, and jam on the table. "Never mind Pappi, Tutti. He's working quite hard nowadays, so we need to be understanding."

Tutti knew Pappi was working hard. Some evenings, he didn't get home until after she was in bed. And on many days, he left in the morning before she and Robbie ate breakfast. But she didn't mind because Mammi was here. And Juffie, too, though Mammi had said that Juffie would be leaving soon. Robbie had cried when he heard, but he was still a baby, after all. Still, even Tutti didn't really understand why Juffie was leaving. Mammi said it was because the Germans had made a new rule: non-Jews were not allowed to work for Jews.

Tutti was starting to get anxious about these new rules. A couple of weeks ago, her mother had sat beside her at bedtime and explained to her that she would be going to a new school this year. She used her happy voice when she told Tutti about it—the same voice she used when she wanted Tutti to eat her carrots. "The new school will be wonderful, *mein kleines Mädchen*. It's so close by—closer than your old school—and your friends Ursula and Rachel will be there."

"But why do I have to go to a new school?" Tutti asked her. "What's wrong with my old school? I want to be with *all* my friends, not just Ursula and Rachel."

"Tuttchen, there are new rules now that the Germans are in charge. You know Jews may only go to Jewish stores and Jewish doctors. Now we have our own schools, too—a school for Jews. Don't you think you'll like that?"

"No, I don't," Tutti sputtered, her tears beginning to fall.

"It's another change, and I know you don't like that. I'm sorry." Mammi's voice was kind and gentle, and she leaned in close to Tutti and smoothed her hair away from her face. "But this way, no one will tease you because you're Jewish, and nobody will get to do things that the other children can't do."

"I won't like it. I won't like it at all," Tutti said.

✤ ✤ ✤

Soon after school began, Mammi and Pappi told her that Jews could no longer go to restaurants, theaters, swimming pools, beaches, zoos, or museums. She would not even be able to visit her favorite place in the world—the Vondelpark.

Tutti wished she could keep herself from crying; she knew it troubled Mammi and Pappi and that the changes weren't their fault. But something in her eyes and heart just had to cry.

✤

mein kleines Mädchen (mine **kline•**ehs **mayt•**chehn): my little girl (German)

6

Stars

May 1942

❧

"Tutti! Robbie! Please come here," Mammi called as she walked through the door.

The children ran to greet her. "Mammi, did you bring us anything? Was there any *stroopwafel* at the bakery today?" They could practically taste their favorite Dutch treat with the caramel filling.

"I'm sorry, *Kinder*. No treats today. Maybe tomorrow." Mammi laid her mesh shopping bag on the table. Visible inside was a small parcel wrapped in brown paper. "Come, let's have a snack. I need to explain something to you."

"What's in the parcel, Mammi?" Tutti asked.

"That's what I want to talk to you about. But first let's eat something." Mammi took an apple from a bowl on the table and began peeling it with a paring knife. She held the handle in her fist and kept her thumb against the side of the blade. As she worked the knife with her right hand, she slowly turned the apple with her left. The entire skin came off in one long strip. Tutti loved to watch her produce these single spiraling apple skins, and she couldn't wait to be old enough to use a sharp knife herself so she could peel an apple just the way her mother did. Mammi cut the apple into pieces and put them on a plate.

This is a photograph of Tutti's first-grade class.
Tutti is standing in the second row from the top, two places
away from her teacher on the right. Tutti's friend
Ursula Heilbut is in the same row, second from the left.

"*Kinder*, look." She took the parcel from her mesh bag and unfolded the brown paper. Inside were pieces of yellow cloth. "Here, you can each hold one."

"What are they, Mammi?" Tutti asked.

"Tutti, can't you see?" said Robbie. "They're stars, of course."

"That's right, Robbie," Mammi interjected. "Do you know what kind of stars?"

"Yellow!" he shouted. "What does it say in the middle?"

"Can you read it, *manneke*?" she asked.

"Does it say 'star?'"

"No, Robbie," Tutti answered. "It says jay-oh-oh-dee—*Jood*. That's Jew. Mammi, what are they for?"

"There's a new rule. All Jews over the age of six have to wear these stars whenever they're not at home," she answered simply.

"I'm only four," Robbie said, holding up four fingers.

"That's right, dear, so you don't have to wear one."

"But what are the stars *for*?" Tutti asked again.

"So they'll know who's Jewish and who isn't," Mammi answered. Tutti could hear the slight catch in her mother's voice.

"How do you wear them?" asked Robbie, as he put one on his head. "Like this?"

"No, silly boy." Mammi smiled but looked away for a moment. "I'll sew them to our clothes. Tutti, can you bring me your coat and two sweaters?"

When Tutti returned, she said, "Mammi, these stars are so the Germans can make sure we're following their rules, aren't they?"

"Yes, *Mädchen*. You're so smart."

"Why don't we just *not* wear them? If we don't wear them, we can pretend we aren't Jewish."

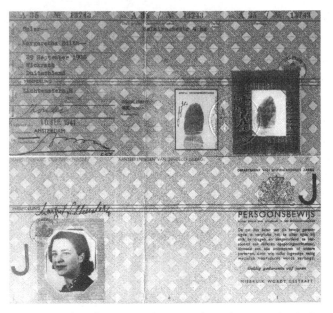

Margret's identification card (required as of January 9, 1942)

"I wish it were that easy, Tuttchen." Mammi sighed. "You know that Pappi and I have identification papers. We must have them with us, and if a policeman asks to see them, we must show them. Have you ever seen mine? Here, take a look at it." She reached into her handbag and pulled out her wallet with her identification. "See the big *J* right next to my picture? That means I'm Jewish. If I ever show the paper and I'm not wearing the star—well, let's just say that would be bad." Again, there was that catch in Mammi's voice.

The yellow star that Jews in the Netherlands were forced to wear

That evening, while Mammi sewed on the badges, Tutti heard her humming a familiar lullaby:

37

Weißt du, wie viel Sternlein stehen
An dem blauen Himmelszelt?
Weißt du, wie viel Wolken gehen
Weit hin über alle Welt?
Gott der Herr hat sie gezählet,
Dass ihm auch nicht eines fehlet
An der ganzen großen Zahl,
An der ganzen großen Zahl.

Can you count the stars that brightly
twinkle in the midnight sky?
Can you count the clouds, so lightly
o'er the meadows floating by?
God, the Lord, doth mark their number,
With His eyes that never slumber;
He hath made them every one,
He hath made them every one.

Mammi's stitches were even, as if she were mending a hem on one of Tutti's dresses. But every once in a while, Tutti saw her shake her head, and the humming would stop.

❧

Jood (yote): Jew (Dutch)

Kinder (**kihn**•dehr): children (German)

Mädchen (**mayt**•chehn): girl (German)

manneke (**mah**•neh•kuh): little man (Dutch)

stroopwafel (**strohp**•wah•fuhl): a caramel-filled waffle (Dutch)

7

Hopeless

❧

"Margret, it's no use," Heinz whispered one night. He had lain in bed for what seemed like hours, waiting for sleep to rescue him from his growing sense of despair.

Margret, who had been awake herself, began to gently stroke his back to comfort him.

"Margret, it's hopeless . . . I thought Egbert would be able to help—to get us false papers. I haven't heard a word." Heinz's voice cracked as he tried to express his worst anxieties. "Why did we come here? Why didn't we move to England? Why . . . why? We're stateless—and the next step is deportation to one of those camps—Westerbork or somewhere worse."

"We didn't know that the Nazis would invade the Netherlands, Heinz. We couldn't have known."

"I think . . . maybe . . ." He couldn't get the words out.

"What?" she asked gently.

"Maybe we should turn on the gas in the oven and die by our own hands."

Margret sat up. "Heinz, have you lost your mind? Why would you say such a thing?"

"Because it's just going to get worse. First the registration, and now those stars we have to wear."

Margret reached over and turned on the bedside lamp.

Heinz and Margret

In its light, she could see her husband's haggard face and anguished expression. "Heinz, that isn't . . . it isn't the right thing . . ."

"But there isn't a scrap of hope." Heinz's voice was nearly a whisper.

Abruptly, Margret climbed out of bed. She couldn't bear to listen to what he was saying for another moment. "You stupid man," she began. "You can't do this. You want to help them? Do you want all the Jews to just kill themselves so that the Nazis can have their Jew-free Europe? What about our children? Do you want to put their heads in the oven, too? Or were you simply planning to leave them to deal with the Germans on their own?" With each question, Margret's voice became louder and harsher.

Heinz looked at his wife in tears. "Margret, I know what's coming. How are we going to survive?"

"We just will, Heinz. That's all." She sat down again and took his hand. "Listen to me. Germany was defeated in 1918, and it won't win this time either. We will get through this. But not like that. Not by thinking about suicide."

Heinz knew that Margret was an optimist, someone who tended to see the positive side of any situation, who believed that every problem had a solution and that bad luck was only temporary. Her optimism was one of the qualities that he had fallen in love with in the first place. He had to find a way to access her strength. He wiped away his tears and felt the pressure of her hand on his, a pressure he tried to return. "I don't know how . . ." he started.

"Together, Heinz. We will get through this together."

8

Spiraling

July 1942

❧

Tutti stretched out on the floor below the window, reading a book. Outside, the sky was still light—it was July, and the sun didn't set until ten o'clock. She could hear the voices of boys playing ball and girls jumping rope.

> *In spin de bocht gaat in*
> *Uit spuit de bocht gaat uit*
> Go in the spinning loop
> Out you go from the loop

She wanted to be outside, too, but that was not allowed. As Mammi had explained to Robbie and her the week before, there was another new rule from the Germans, called a curfew: all Jews had to be in their own homes from eight o'clock at night until six o'clock the next morning.

Earlier that evening, at exactly ten minutes to eight, Mammi had come out on the stoop and called, "Come inside, Tuttchen!"

"But Rachel, Etty, and I are having a jump rope contest, Mammi. We need to finish. Please, can't we play a little longer?"

"You can play outside again tomorrow. Rachel has to go home, too. Her mother will be coming for her any minute." And seconds later, Rachel's mother appeared, grabbed her daughter wordlessly by the arm, and pulled her away.

Without Rachel, the contest couldn't continue, and Tutti had reluctantly followed her mother inside. But how unfair it seemed. While other children were still enjoying the summer breeze—still shouting and laughing with each other—Tutti had to stay inside in her stuffy, cramped room.

She wished the new apartment, where they had moved a few weeks ago, weren't so small. Mammi and Pappi occupied one bedroom, Robbie and Tutti shared another, and Muttchen and Okkie, Pappi's parents, slept in the living room. The six of them made do with one bathroom. "Pappi is trying to save money now," Mammi had said when Tutti asked why they had to leave De Lairessestraat and move to Diezestraat. "This new apartment is cheaper. It's small, but we're lucky to be together."

Tutti knew that sometimes Mammi didn't feel so lucky. In such close quarters, she could often hear Mammi and Pappi talking at night about other relatives. She knew that Uncle Bobby and Aunt Tineke were missing, and that Mammi was terribly worried about what had become of them. They had planned to sneak out of the Netherlands— had paid a boat captain to smuggle them across the North Sea—but somebody alerted the Gestapo, and they had been arrested.

"If only they had managed to make it to England!" she heard Mammi saying tearfully one evening. Tutti didn't mean to eavesdrop, but the sound carried readily through the apartment's thin walls. She knew they were talking about Uncle Bobby again.

There was a pause while Pappi said something Tutti couldn't hear. Then there was Mammi's voice again, firmer now: "I know, but it's just a rumor. There is no definite information. I won't assume the worst. I must believe he is alive unless I find out something different."

The next morning, Mammi got breakfast for the family as cheerfully as ever. When Robbie balked at eating his hot cereal, Mammi was as patient with him as she always was.

"Mammi," Tutti began, as she helped her mother clear the breakfast dishes. She wanted to know about Uncle Bobby—what the rumor was. "I heard you talking about Uncle Bobby and Aunt Tineke. Are they all right?" Mammi had the water running and didn't seem to hear the question. "Mammi?"

"Run along and play now, Tuttchen," Muttchen interrupted. "I'll help your mother with the dishes."

Tutti realized that this was a topic her mother didn't want to discuss. She would have to wait to find out about her aunt and uncle.

☘

Muttchen (**muhtch•**ehn): Granny (Tutti and Robbie's paternal grandmother's name was Jenny, but they called her Muttchen) (German)

9

Something to Hold On To

June 20, 1943

❧

The situation for Jews in the Netherlands continued to deterio-rate that summer. On July 15, 1942, more than 1,100 Jewish refugees living in the Netherlands were transported to Auschwitz-Birkenau—one of the three main extermination camps in Poland.

By April of the next year, Jews in the Netherlands had been forced to live all together in Amsterdam or in one of the two transit camps, Westerbork or Vught. And frequent raids in Jewish neighborhoods were setting everyone's nerves on edge.

❧   ❧   ❧

Heinz was incredulous. *I can't believe what I'm reading.* "Baggage Shipping to the Camps: What One Needs to Know." *A whole page about what one needs to know! So many restrictions.*

"It is expressly forbidden to put uncensored letters in packages to camps." *Are Bobby and Tineke in one of those awful camps?*

"You are urgently advised to have all papers and documents with you." *My papers. Are they in order? Yes, here in my pocket.*

"People who have to go to Westerbork or Vught should have two blankets."

"Margret, make sure each rucksack has two blankets," Heinz said without looking up.

"Heinz, do you think we have a dozen extra blankets?" It was Jenny, his mother, who answered. The more anxious her son became, the more nervous she felt. "How can we have six rucksacks packed at all times with two extra blankets each? Besides, we won't have to go anywhere. You're on the Jewish Council. We have an exemption."

"I'm not on the Jewish Council. I'm only on an advisory committee. And yes, we have an exemption. But I don't trust it. Plenty of people with exemptions have been picked up."

Calmly, Margret offered a solution. "It's June. It's too hot for blankets, anyway. Let's pack them and just sleep with sheets. We won't need blankets on the beds for months.

Heinz's Jewish Council registration card

By then, this whole war should be over. Come, Jenny, let's take care of the rucksacks."

Before he got into bed that evening, Heinz performed his nightly ritual: double-checked that all his papers were in his billfold and made sure that the emergency bags were packed and by the front door. He was grateful that his wife was resourceful and willing to keep everything prepared. For a whole year, she had kept the children's bags ready with properly fitting clothes, and she regularly updated the packed food so it wouldn't spoil.

The last part of the ritual was checking in on the children. Then Heinz and Margret headed to bed, and the apartment was soon quiet.

꽃   꽃   꽃

In the middle of the night, Heinz woke with a start. "Margret, do you hear that?"

"I don't hear a thing. You must be dreaming."

"No, I heard something." Heinz got out of bed and went to the open window. As he pulled back the curtain a fraction of an inch, he saw trucks arriving at the end of the block. SS troops began to spill out of them, and were soon joined by the Dutch police. Heinz closed the window and let the curtain fall back in place. "Margret, wake my parents. It's a raid."

Within seconds, soldiers were banging on front doors up and down the block, and a loudspeaker was squawking: "All Jews must report now. All Jews outside immediately! You may each bring one bag. All Jews outside immediately!"

Okkie, Jenny, Heinz, and Margret stood in their slippered feet in the living room. Heinz saw Okkie and Jenny's dazed expressions—saw that Margret looked anxious but resolute. Both his wife and mother, he noted, were holding their robes with clenched fists over their hearts, as if the thin cotton could protect them from what was happening.

Heinz went to the window and peered out a slit in the curtains.

"How close are they?" demanded Okkie.

"About 50 meters," whispered Heinz.

"Do you have your papers?" Okkie asked.

"Yes, I have them." He did his best to muster a confident tone for his father, but his heart was pounding furiously. They would probably be safe, he told himself. He was an advisor to the Jewish Council, after all. In any case, he would be exempt from arrest because of his work in the metals business, and he had been told his position would protect his family, as well.

Heinz was glued to the window. He saw two men, neighbors, running across the rooftops on the other side of the street. He silently prayed for the safe escape of those brave souls.

"Mammi, what's happening?" Robbie was standing in the doorway rubbing his sleepy eyes. Tutti stood silently behind him clutching a doll.

"Shush, *Kinder*. There are soldiers outside. We need to be very quiet right now." Margret put an arm around each child and ushered them back to bed. Heinz could hear her singing to them in a whisper.

Then a moment later, the police pounded loudly on the door. "Open! *Politie!*" The three Dutch police burst in before the door was completely open. "Jews live here!" they shouted.

"*Ja*, but I have an exemption from the Jewish Council." Heinz kept his voice steady but his hand trembled as he held out his papers.

"You are Heinz Lichtenstern?"

A page from the Amsterdam Jewish Council guide listing the Advisory Board for non-Dutch Jews, including H. Lichtenstern

"Ja."

"And this old woman, this is your wife?" he asked, looking at Jenny in disbelief.

"No, this is my mother. My wife is in the bedroom with the children." Heinz immediately regretted saying this. What had he done? He was hoping to keep attention away from Tutti and Robbie.

"Een minuut." The policemen took the papers and left.

Okkie went to the window. One policeman was holding the papers and talking to the German soldiers in the street. He turned back toward the building and this time entered the apartment without knocking.

"You and you," he pointed to Okkie and Jenny. "Be in the square at Daniël Willinkplein in fifteen minutes. Anyone who doesn't report will be shot."

"But I was told my family would be exempt!" insisted Heinz.

The Dutch policeman's voice had the slightest hint of compassion. "Yes, you, your wife, your children. But not your parents. They must report." An SS soldier appeared behind him in the entryway. Abruptly, his tone changed back. "I have my orders." And he left.

"Muttchen, Papa . . . they said *my family* . . ." Heinz's voice trailed off.

Jenny reached out her arms to her son.

With only fifteen minutes, they had to move quickly. There was a flurry of hugs and kisses and goodbyes. Margret grabbed some food—a loaf of bread and a hunk of cheese— and pushed it into her mother-in-law's bag. Heinz put a pencil and some paper into his father's coat pocket. "Write

Jenny, Flo, and Okkie (presumably, Louis took the photo)
at a café in Germany (1933)

to us. Tell us where you are. I'll . . . I don't know what, but I'll do something."

"I will, son."

What Margret didn't know that night was that raids were happening all over the city, and her parents, Flo and Louis Spier, were also being forced to leave their home.

Heinz watched out the window as his parents walked away carrying their small bags. It was hard to bear, but he had to keep looking. On a whim, just before they were out of earshot, he whistled to them. *"Phweet, Phweet, Phweet, Phweet, Phweeeeeeee!"* It was the five-note whistle his family always used to find each other in crowds—something he and his brother had been taught as boys and that he had taught his own children. It might be something to hold on to during their journey.

❧

een minuut (ayn mih•**noot**): one minute (Dutch)

Okkie (**aw**•kee): a nickname for Oscar

politie (poh•**leet**•see): police (Dutch)

10

Masquerade

❧

Two weeks had passed since the raid that took away Okkie and Muttchen and Louis and Flo, and the family was jittery.

One afternoon, while Tutti and Robbie were setting up a game of hopscotch on the sidewalk in front of their building, they suddenly dropped their chalk, raced upstairs, and burst through the front door, slamming it behind them.

"Pappi, there's a German soldier outside," said Tutti while she tried to catch her breath.

"He just got out of a big car," added Robbie.

Heinz went to the window. A black Mercedes Benz was parked outside 29 Diezestraat. But there were no soldiers in sight.

"Tutti, how many soldiers did you see?" he asked.

"Two—the driver and a man with a box."

A loud knock silenced Tutti.

Heinz whispered, "Margret, take the children into the bedroom. Quickly!" Then he went to the door. "Who's there?"

"*Abwehr!* Open up!" came the deep voice.

Heinz held his breath as he tried to remember everywhere he had been in the past few days. Had he done something to anger the authorities? Was he under suspicion for some indiscretion? Had Egbert tried to buy him a passport . . .

and now were they both going to be shot? He was shaking as he opened the door.

The man who stood there was heavyset, with a round face and a pronounced widow's peak. He held a flat box under his arm. Heinz exhaled in relief and felt his heartbeat return to normal.

"*Um Gottes Willen*, Friedrich! You scared me half to death. Come in." Heinz closed the door behind his friend, Baron Friedrich von Oppenheim, and called out, "Margret, *alles gut!* It's Friedrich von Oppenheim!"

Margret emerged from the bedroom, and Heinz couldn't tell from the look on her face whether she planned to hug their friend or slap him. "Friedrich, you gave us such a scare. Why?"

"Heinz, Margret, sit down. I have a good reason."

Baron Friedrich von Oppenheim was a banker from Cologne and had known the Lichtensterns for years. He was a good friend of Heinz's boss, Meno Lissauer, the owner of Oxyde, and helped him escape from the Netherlands in September 1940, just four months after the Germans had invaded. He himself was one-quarter Jewish.

"I'm so sorry I had to frighten you that way, but I want this to look real. I want the whole neighborhood to be talking and saying how the *Abwehr* came and picked you up. This way, nobody will be searching for you."

"Friedrich, what in God's name are you talking about?" asked Heinz, as he leapt from his chair.

"I have a plan. You have blond hair and blue eyes. You're tall and handsome. You're German. You don't look like a Jew. You could pass as an Aryan any day of the week." As von Oppenheim talked, he seemed to grow more and more excited.

Baron Friedrich von Oppenheim

"Friedrich, I don't understand," interrupted Margret.

"Please, give me a chance to explain." He opened the box that he'd been holding on his lap. Inside was a neatly folded black uniform with shiny metal buttons—an SS uniform.

"It'll fit you," said Friedrich, as he held the jacket against Heinz's shoulders. "I have a car and a driver downstairs. Everyone will think you've been arrested, but I will bring all of you to Germany. Heinz, I can set you up as an SS officer. You can play the part until the war ends. You and your family will be safe, hiding right in plain sight."

"Friedrich, that sounds crazy." Heinz started pacing around the room. "I don't think I can do that."

"Of course you can. I was able to get Lissauer to Brazil, but that isn't an option anymore. Hitler is becoming more determined. He has pledged that all the Jews will disappear from Europe. You must do this. The war will end and then you can go back to being Heinz Lichtenstern, the metals trader. But for now, we'll make up a name. You'll be . . . you will be Heinz Neumann, SS *Untersturmführer*. That's it! Heinz Neumann—a *new man*." Baron von Oppenheim looked pleased with both his plan and his play on words.

Heinz paced around the room, looking at Margret for guidance. Her eyes were twice their normal size and all the color had drained from her cheeks. Then he turned to his friend, a banker from Cologne in a Nazi uniform, and said, "Friedrich, I know you're taking a risk to do this, but I can't. I'm not a good actor. I can't go to Germany and pretend I'm a Nazi. I've never even held a gun! And what if I have to give some order that endangers Jews? I couldn't. I just couldn't."

"Heinz, I'm begging you. Things are getting worse. Your status as a metals trader won't protect you forever," pleaded von Oppenheim.

"I'm sorry, Friedrich. I can't."

Quietly, the two men walked to the door and then turned and tightly embraced one another. Friedrich von Oppenheim knew what was at stake for the Lichtensterns, and Heinz knew what his friend had put on the line by coming. He had to find some way to protect his family. But by pretending to be a Nazi officer? That he couldn't do—ever.

Abwehr (ahp•vehr): German Military Intelligence (German)

alles gut (ahl•luhs goot): all's well (German)

11

Their Next Move

September 16, 1943

❧

That fall, Margret told Tutti that the family would be moving again. "We'll need to pack soon, so let's decide what to take with us," she said.

"Can't we take everything?" asked Tutti. "I don't want to leave anything behind."

A year ago, when they had left their large apartment for the one they lived in now on Diezestraat, those decisions had been wrenching.

"I know you would like to bring everything, sweetheart, but the new apartment will be much smaller. We can only bring what's important. Please pack this bag with your clothes. Don't bother with anything that is already getting small."

"I don't care about my clothes. I just want to have my dolls."

"You can bring one doll, Tuttchen."

"Only one? But—" Tutti frowned and stopped herself. She knew she mustn't argue with her mother, but what Mammi wanted was impossible. She burst out, "I can't leave them! I need them!"

"Tutti, the new apartment is very small. And we have to carry all of our belongings—like cooking pots and blankets—with us. We can't take our things in a car or on the tram. We have to walk." As she often did, Margret spoke gently but firmly. She hated to put her children through these changes, but there was no alternative. "There simply isn't room for many toys."

"If the new apartment isn't nice, why are we moving, Mammi?" asked Tutti.

Margret sighed. "Because the Germans said we have to. We have to live in one of the Jewish neighborhoods."

"But what will happen to my dolls? I can't leave them!" A tear rolled down Tutti's cheek.

Margret knelt in front of her daughter and took both her hands. "Tutti, here's what we'll do. I have some things that are very important to me—like our furniture and some of our paintings. Pappi gave them to his friend Adriaan Vos when we left De Lairessestraat. He said he would keep our possessions safe for us until we come home. We can ask him to take care of your dolls, too."

"Will he be careful with them? Sometimes they get scared."

"Yes, he'll be careful. I promise."

"Are you sure there's only room for one? What if I take two?"

"Just one," said Margret softly, as she squeezed her daughter's hands.

That afternoon, Tutti had to make a difficult decision. She had two favorite dolls—Roosje and Beatrix. Roosje had a bright pink dress with small yellow flowers on the collar. Her hair was blonde and Tutti had put a bow in it. Beatrix was a baby doll, and Tutti had named her after the little granddaughter of the Dutch queen, who was the same age as Robbie. Finally, she decided on Roosje. She was big enough to hug and to sit on Tutti's lap, but she wasn't too big.

The next day, they carried their suitcases to the new apartment on Afrikanerplein in the Transvaalbuurt—one of the last neighborhoods where Jews were allowed to live. They had to carry everything to the third floor. One after another, they dragged their suitcases up the steep and narrow staircase, angling their bags around the landings, breathing heavily by the time they reached their door.

At last, Pappi turned the key in the lock, and with two hands on the suitcase handle, he pushed in the door with his shoulder. The rooms were tiny. In the main room there was a lamp with a ripped shade and an old couch with one leg shorter than the others. It was propped up with a pile of books. The two bedrooms were in the back. One had ugly brown walls and the other had a large stain on the floor.

"Tutti, Robbie, you two will share this room," said Mammi, using what Tutti thought of as her happy voice. It was a voice that Tutti had gotten to know well over the past three years.

"But Mammi, there's just one bed in here," complained Tutti.

"It's okay," answered her mother. "We'll find another bed somehow. Until then, you can share with Robbie."

"When we get another bed, can we put it over that stain on the floor?" asked Tutti.

"Yes, that's an excellent idea."

Now Tutti understood why they'd had to leave most of their things behind. But she hadn't expected how lonely and strange the apartment would seem without her family's familiar books and pictures and knickknacks.

12

Look!

❧

"Come, Tutti. Look," Robbie begged. He had his nose and two hands pressed against the window, trying to see what was responsible for the shouting and the other noises coming from the street.

Tutti didn't really want to look, but she didn't want Robbie to call her a baby, either. After all, she was eight and he was only five. She knew they were supposed to stay away from the window in their tiny apartment on Afrikanerplein—Mammi had told them that repeatedly— but she decided to peek for just a minute so he would stop pestering her.

What she saw was frightening and confusing. There were men, women, and children gathered across the street. Families were clutching each other. Soldiers seemed to be yelling and pushing people into trucks. Police dogs strained against their short leashes, barking and baring their teeth. Tutti didn't want to watch, but she somehow couldn't turn away. Her feet were stuck; her eyes were fixated on the tumult across the street. Without realizing it, she hugged Roosje to her chest in the same desperate way that the women outside were clinging to their babies.

Tutti tried to make out their faces. Was that Ursula? Ursula had been in her class at school. And was that Mr. and

Mrs. Joël, who lived downstairs? The commotion made it impossible to tell exactly what was happening, but it looked like people were being taken away. *Was* that Mrs. Joël? She seemed to be carrying a cat. Tutti didn't think the Joëls even had a cat. It was hard to see, so she pressed herself against the window to get a better view.

A moment later, someone grabbed Tutti from behind. She screamed and dropped Roosje, then clutched at the curtain. It was the soldiers—they had come for her, and she was going to be taken away in one of those terrible trucks! "Mammi!" she screamed. She knew she wasn't supposed to stand by the window! If she had listened to Mammi instead of letting Robbie talk her into looking, then this wouldn't be happening. She would never disobey Mammi again, would never misbehave. If only they wouldn't take her away!

Someone spun her roughly around, but the person she came face-to-face with wasn't a soldier. It was their neighbor, Mrs. Oberländer, who was yelling something. Tutti was so confused that she could barely stand, let alone comprehend what was being said to her. But finally she understood the words: "Don't stand by the window with that pink doll!"

As Tutti let go of the curtain, the woman snatched her up, shut the curtains, and carried her away.

"Mammi, Mammi!" Tutti could hardly get the words out between her sobs. She didn't know if her tears were coming from fear or relief. "I just wanted to see who they were taking. I thought I saw Ursula down there."

"I understand. Shh, shh, stop crying, Tuttchen. Roosje's clothes are bright pink, and the soldiers might have noticed them in the window. That's why when Mrs. Oberländer saw you standing there with her, she got worried, that's all. I'm sorry I didn't notice first."

"No, I'm sorry, Mammi," Tutti said, interrupting, and doing her best to stop crying. "It was Robbie's idea to watch." She didn't care if she was tattling.

"Listen to me, Tuttchen." Mammi's tone was less soothing now and more serious. "I don't think anybody saw you, this time. But they could have. Remember, we want to blend in and not give the soldiers any reason to look up at our window."

"I understand, Mammi. I won't do it again."

Tutti poked Robbie on the way back to their room. It was all *his* fault.

13

The Letter

Late September 1943

❖

Heinz's hands shook as he opened the envelope. His greatest fear was being realized: it was a letter from the *Sicherheitspolizei,* ordering him and his family to report the following day to police headquarters.

"Margret! Margret! Come here!" Heinz demanded. He paced the tiny room and waved the letter back and forth.

"What is it?" Margret hurried into the living room. But when she saw the letter, she knew.

"We've been called up," he told her. "They're sending us to Westerbork."

Margret sank down on the couch, momentarily overcome. Then she said, "What about the children?"

"They want all of us to report. All four of us!"

"We can't bring them to a place like that, Heinz. We just *can't,*" she insisted.

"What choice do we have? If we don't report, they'll arrest us." Heinz walked to the window, glancing out to the same spot where Tutti had watched the raid a few days ago, and then walked to the kitchen to peer out the rear window. Back and forth, back and forth he paced. Finally, he stopped and gazed into Margret's teary eyes. "We have to *go* somewhere."

"Yes, but where? My brother tried to escape to England and that ended in disaster. We don't know if he's dead or in one of those camps. Where can we go?"

Heinz wasn't listening. He was thinking out loud: "If we report, we're doomed. But if we don't report, they'll come here in the middle of the night. We're sitting ducks. We need to find someplace to hide."

"But where? Whom can we trust?"

Heinz and Margret were fully aware of the dangers of going into hiding. They would be at the complete mercy of others. There were crooks who took advantage of Jews, promising safety for large sums of money, only to break their promises. There were people who turned Jews over to the Gestapo for the bounty of seven guilders. But there were also courageous people who were willing to risk being arrested or even killed to help Jews in need.

"Margret, I'm going out. I need to see what I can arrange. I'll be back as soon as I can. Pack—a few sets of clothes for everyone. And gather up all the ration cards." Heinz grabbed his hat and took the stairs two at a time on his way down to the street.

✤ ✤ ✤

When Heinz came home, he was only slightly calmer than when he had left. "Margret, Margret! Come," he called. He quickly explained that he had talked with Egbert de Jong from the office phone and made a plan. "Margret, we're going underground. Egbert has begun making the arrangements already." Bobby Klopfer, who worked for Oxyde too, had agreed to hide them. He was Jewish, but his wife, Adele, was Christian, so they were exempt from deportation. Their house would be safe.

He didn't tell Margret what Egbert had said about the camp in Westerbork. He didn't tell her that it was a transit camp, a way station for people being sent to one of the terrible camps in the East—Germany or Poland. And he didn't tell her that old people, women, and children were the first to be sent away.

"Heinz, I have the bags packed. Do we have to go now, or can we explain it to the children tonight and go tomorrow?" Margret asked.

"We have to leave now, before curfew. But suitcases will look suspicious. I'm sorry I told you to pack them," he said nervously. "We'll just have to wear as many clothes as possible. Dress in lots of layers. Robbie can put on a couple of pairs of pants, and I am sure Tutti can wear a dress on top of her skirt."

"We can take rucksacks, right? Small ones? I'll pack food," added Margret.

As always, he admired her calm resourcefulness. "*Ja*. And pack your jewelry—all of it. We can use it to bribe someone in a pinch. We need to leave as soon as possible. It'll take at least an hour to walk across town to Michelangelostraat with the children, and we need to get there before the eight o'clock curfew."

Quietly, Margret explained to the children what they needed to do. To Tutti, putting on layer after layer seemed like a crazy game of dress-up. Robbie teased her that she looked fat, and she laughed at how the layers made him waddle. Still, she understood from the urgency in Mammi's voice that this was no game.

"How long will we stay with the Klopfers, Mammi?" Tutti asked as they made their way down the narrow stairs.

"We're going to stay with them for a while," answered Margret.

"But why? Why can't we stay here?" asked Robbie.

"We don't want the police to take us away from Amsterdam," explained Heinz. "When they come, our apartment will be empty, and then maybe they'll simply forget about us."

As they got close to Michelangelostraat, Margret paused at the canal, pointing out the sights—the beautiful elm trees beginning to turn gold, the green-brown water in the canal that was never quite still, and the ducks paddling in slow circles. Heinz realized that she didn't know how long it would be until the children could run and play outside again, and she wanted to make sure they had beautiful images of the outdoors to carry them through their time in hiding.

"*Kinderen,* Margret, let's get inside," Heinz said after a moment. "It's almost eight o'clock."

❧

kinderen (kihn•duh•ruhn): children (Dutch)

Sicherheitspolizei (zikh•uhr•hites•poh•leet•tzahy): Security Police (German)

14

Out of Sight

❧

Bobby Klopfer met them at the door and led them to a small room on the fourth floor. In this part of town, the apartment buildings had been built for well-to-do families, with attics designed to house people's servants. Ten or twenty years ago, there would have been a maid or a cook living in this room. Now it had four cots, a small table, and a sink. There was a tiny bathroom down the hall, which Klopfer explained they could use whenever he let them know the coast was clear.

Tutti was tired from the walk and overheated from her layered clothing, and she looked around in confusion. "Mammi, why are we here?" she asked.

"I already explained that to you, Tutti."

"I know why we left home. But you said we were visiting the Klopfers. They have a nice place with a big chandelier in the living room. I remember it. This isn't their house."

"Oh, Tuttchen. This *is* their house. They live on the second floor. This is their storage room."

"Why can't we be in the nice rooms?" asked Robbie.

"Because if anyone visits, they'll know we're here. It has to be a secret. As a matter of fact, I want you both to take your shoes off right now." Margret bent down and started to untie Robbie's shoes.

An attic room on Michelangelostraat,
probably the one where Tutti and her family hid (2015)

"Why do we need to take our shoes off, Mammi?" asked Tutti.

"Well, Mr. and Mrs. Klopfer live on the second floor. The Werthauers live on the third floor. That means our floor is their ceiling. I don't want them to hear us walking around up here. Socks are much quieter. As long as we are living here, we won't wear shoes."

Tutti realized that it was another strange new rule. She tried to remember them all: the stars, the Jewish schools, the curfew, and now no shoes. She took them off and walked over to the window in her stocking feet.

"No, Tutti." Heinz intercepted her before she could open the curtain. "These curtains must stay shut."

"Can't I watch the ducks in the canal?"

"If you can see out, then somebody can see in. And *nobody* can know we're here." Her father wore his sternest expression.

"But it's dark here," said Robbie. He was tired too, so it came out as a whine.

It was Margret who answered. "It isn't dark," she said. "We have a small lamp, and we have each other. We have to be very quiet. Nobody can know we're here."

❧   ❧   ❧

Every day in the attic was the same: Bobby or Adele Klopfer would come by with food and the newspaper and would spend a few minutes talking with Heinz and Margret. But the children had no toys or books, and they couldn't make noise. They took to folding the newspapers to make hats and boats and swords, and Margret told them whatever fairy tales she could remember, and even made up fanciful stories.

One day when Bobby came upstairs, he told Heinz that there had been a large raid in the Transvaalbuurt, right after they left. They had gone into hiding in the nick of time. Among the 5,000 Jews taken away that night were Heinz's neighbors Leopold and Lilli Oberländer and his friends Josef and Else Sax.

Heinz saw to it that the curtain stayed closed at all times, but he liked to stand next to the window. He could just see a little slit of the street if he angled his head the right way. He spent hours watching and waiting for the Germans to come pick them up.

When Bobby or Adele dropped by in the evening with dinner, he interrogated them. Had anyone been asking about the Lichtensterns? Had there been any raids nearby? Who else knew they were here?

At night, he lay in bed listening to the sounds around him. Each car driving by, each creaky floorboard on the stairs, and every shout from the street made him jump. He couldn't relax.

He watched the children sleep and wished that he could be as peaceful as they were, but how could he be? He was putting his whole family at risk by hiding. What if they were found?

15

Special Delivery

Late October 1943

❧

One morning, about three weeks into their life in the attic, Bobby Klopfer brought Heinz a large envelope.

"This was delivered to the office today," Bobby said, grinning.

Heinz opened the envelope warily, though Bobby's smile was reassuring, and removed a small black book. It was the size of a personal diary, but much thinner, and contained a single sheet of thick white paper, folded like a map. It appeared to be blank, but when Heinz flipped over the page, he saw four familiar faces.

Heinz hugged his friend and kissed Margret. Then he laughed out loud. Bobby had brought them a family passport. Heinz hadn't been this hopeful in such a long time.

"Pappi, what's so funny?" Tutti asked. She looked at the little book and tried to make out the words. "*Au nom de la Répub*—? Mammi, what does this say? I can't read it."

"*Au nom de la République de Paraguay,*" Margret read in a genuinely happy voice.

"What does that mean?" asked Robbie.

"It means, 'On behalf of the Republic of Paraguay.'"

"What else?" asked Tutti.

"*Le consul de la République de Paraguay à Berne. Invite par les présents toutes les autorités et les employés—*"

"It doesn't make any sense, Mammi," interrupted Robbie. "Is it Dutch or German?"

"Neither. It's French!" Margret beamed. "It says that the consulate in Bern, Switzerland, has given us a Paraguayan passport!"

"What's Paraguayan?" asked Tutti. It must be something very good to make Pappi laugh and Mammi smile this way.

Pappi explained, "Paraguay is a country in South America. This says we are citizens of that country. And the best part about it is that Paraguay is not part of this war!"

"So we're going to South America?" asked Robbie.

"No. But the Nazis will have to respect that we're not stateless Jews anymore. They don't want other countries to be angry with them."

Robbie pointed to all the pictures. "That's me and Tutti and Mammi and Pappi."

"I see Pappi's name there and Mammi's there," said Tutti. "But where's my name?"

"You're right here." Margret pointed at the phrase *deux enfants.* "That means 'two children.'"

While Margret was explaining everything on the passport, Heinz spoke to Bobby in a whisper. "How did you get it?"

"I didn't. It was Egbert de Jong."

"De Jong! Thank goodness for de Jong. I knew he would find a way," said Heinz.

"He worked with Jakob Jorysch in Basel. They paid the consul in Bern. With the money you gave Egbert, he was able to issue about thirty of these for Oxyde families. Egbert brought this one to the office today! Jorysch hasn't sent them all. To avoid the possibility of their being intercepted all at once, he's sending them one at a time. I was told that Mau Hanemann has one, too."

"That's wonderful news. Let's hope they *all* get through," Heinz said to Bobby. Then, turning to Margret, he smiled and said, "Let's go home."

Margret was caught off guard, and she looked at him questioningly. "Is that wise, Heinz?"

"We aren't really safe here," he whispered, not wanting the children to hear. "There have been searches all over

The Lichtenstern family's Paraguayan passport

the neighborhood. The Nazis are aware that because many Jewish families used to live here, some residents might be sheltering friends. I heard a raid from the direction of Minervalaan just last night. If we're found here, we'll be shot, and Bobby and Adele will be arrested—or worse—for hiding us. But if we go home and turn ourselves in, we might have a chance."

Heinz seemed to have thought this through carefully. Returning home was risky, Margret knew, but so was life in the attic. And it was even more difficult for the children! The thought of breathing fresh air again and walking along the canal like a human being was powerfully appealing. "Let's go, Heinz," she said simply.

But Heinz's mood was buoyant. "So, Señora Lichtenstern!" he boomed. "You are now a citizen of Paraguay! The Nazis may have sent for us, but they didn't know we had *this!*" Heinz held the passport high over his head. "I'll bring the passport to the Office of Jewish Emigration. They'll have to take it into account—and then we won't have to go anywhere!"

✤   ✤   ✤

The next day, Heinz and Margret helped Tutti and Robbie put on all their clothes, and together they walked back to their little apartment in the Transvaalbuurt neighborhood. Their mood was far different from what it had been three weeks earlier, when Pappi's anxiety had been palpable, and when putting on so many clothes had felt strange and comical. This time they were going back to their apartment—where they might be able to stay for good, now that they had the Paraguayan passport.

With Margret, Tutti, and Robbie safely back on Afrikanerplein, Heinz immediately left for the Jewish emigration office. He patted his pocket repeatedly to assure himself that he had the new passport, its letter of notarization, and the letter ordering the family to report. Pausing briefly outside the door, he reminded himself to be firm and confident. He needed to make this work. He had to keep his family from being sent to the camps.

As he approached the desk with the uniformed clerk, he took off his hat and handed over his paperwork. He didn't say a word. He was afraid anything he said would work against him. After all, he was supposed to have reported three and a half weeks ago.

"You are Heinz Lichtenstern?" asked the clerk in a short clip.

"*Jawohl*," answered Heinz.

"You were ordered to report on September 29. It is now October 24." The clerk pulled out a book from the desk and flipped through the pages. "We've been looking for you."

"*Jawohl*."

"Where are the others? This paper has four names." The clerk's voice was mechanical. Heinz could tell that he had had this conversation countless times over the past year.

"My wife and children are at home. I wanted to come alone and show you our passport," he said.

"What do I care about a passport?" The clerk pushed the passport away. He didn't open it. He barely glanced at it. He just kept examining his register. "Here. Twenty-nine September. That is when you should have been here. You and your wife and two children."

"But I'm a Paraguayan citizen. I have the papers. See? I even have a letter of notarization."

"You are a Jew. Your wife is a Jew. Your children are Jews. You must report. Today. Get your family. If you are not all at the Joodsche Schouwburg by three o'clock, I will send the police to arrest you."

"But if you will just look at this!" Heinz pleaded, pushing the passport back to the clerk.

The clerk stared at him with dark, indifferent eyes. He didn't take the passport. He wouldn't even look at it. "Listen. I don't care about passports. I have my orders. You are on the list of people who are supposed to report. You need to get your family and bring them to the Jewish Theater, and you need to do it now. Maybe someone there will look at your passport. I don't care about passports. All I care about is that the people here in my register are checked off as having been accounted for. Do you understand?"

"*Ja, ich verstehe.*"

Yes, I understand—perfectly. Heinz had thought that the Jewish Council papers would protect his parents. He had thought that the passport would protect Margret and the children. He had been wrong on both counts. Now he had to go home and explain to Margret that he had failed.

Margret took the news without a word and quickly packed a bag for each person. Heinz saw her wiping away tears while she gathered the necessary items. He knew she didn't blame him, but still he had to explain—had to tell her how unreasonable the clerk had been, how he had threatened to send the police if they didn't report by three o'clock. He paced back and forth, his face red and his fists clenched. He was angry with the clerk who wouldn't look at his papers. But mostly he was angry with himself for leaving their hiding place—for thinking that the passport would save them. He had let his family down.

🌱

jawohl (yah•**vohl**): yes (German)

16

Hold Robbie's Hand

❧

Tutti watched her mother pack their bags. Each person had a few changes of clothes, some food, and two blankets. Mammi and Pappi also had the important family papers in their rucksacks. Then they left and headed up Krugerstraat. As they walked by Retiefstraat, Tutti recognized it. "Mammi, that's Oma Flo and Opa Louis's street, isn't it?"

"Yes, Tutti. You're right." Mammi pointed down the narrow street and reminded the children which doorway had led to her parents' house four months ago—before the raid that took them away. "But they don't live there anymore."

The children lingered as they passed the Oosterpark. Mammi drew their attention to the large grassy field and the flower beds where the tulips had once bloomed but were now dormant. She told Tutti and Robbie how the bulbs were under the dirt, getting ready to go to sleep for the winter, and how they would bloom again in the spring. As they crossed the bridge over the Muidergracht canal, Tutti stopped to look for ducks and seagulls.

"Mammi, can we feed the ducks?" asked Robbie.

"No, Robbie, I'm sorry," Pappi said. "We have to report to the Schouwburg."

"Heinz . . . this might be the last . . . Please, they don't understand." Tutti noticed how sad Mammi's eyes were as she spoke to Pappi.

"We can't feed the birds. We need everything we have for ourselves," said Pappi.

Mammi gently took the children's hands and led them away from the bridge. She talked about the ducks and how birds travel in flocks and help each other by taking turns in the front of the "V."

They walked silently, hand-in-hand, for another five blocks until they reached the Schouwburg. Tutti thought the theater was beautiful. She marveled at the cream-colored building with its grand arched doors and columns along the front. As she looked up, she saw many windows and a carving of people at the top of the façade.

The entryway had big double doors and the front hall was made of white marble. She imagined men and women going there on dates. Ladies with lace gloves and diamond brooches would hold the arms of their husbands, who would be dressed in suits with shiny shoes. Once seated, they would enjoy the shows, and laugh and clap until it was time to go home again.

"Mammi, have you ever been here before?"

"Yes, Tutti. Pappi and I have been here many times."

"Please tell me about the shows."

"Tutti, the last show your father and I saw was with Max Ehrlich. Do you remember Mr. and Mrs. Ehrlich? They used to come to our house for dinner."

"No, Mammi, I don't."

"Mr. Ehrlich is the man who pretended to steal your nose and then pull it out of your ear when you were little," Mammi said.

"Oh, he's such a funny man! Can you tell me some of his jokes?"

"Not now, Tutti. Right now I need you to do something for me."

"What is it, Mammi?"

"Hold your brother's hand. Pappi and I have to talk to the registration people, and I need you and Robbie right here beside us. You can't let him wander off. I need the two of you right next to me the whole time."

As she was ushered inside, Tutti's daydreams of concert-going couples vanished. The room contained the anguish of the tens of thousands of frightened and battered Jews who had already passed through its doors, and all Tutti wanted was to go outside again. The windows were boarded up. There were small red emergency lights on the wall. Other than that, it was dark and frightening.

"Mammi . . . I want to go back outside." Tutti dropped her rucksack by her feet and looked around the room. She tucked her nose under her collar to avoid the stuffy smell and watched her tears as they rolled down her coat.

"Tutti, I know this is hard. Here, take my handkerchief. Just be sure you keep a hold of Robbie's hand."

When it was their turn for registration, Pappi handed the Paraguayan passport to the clerk. The soldier skimmed the papers, handed them back while he made a 'harrumph' sound, and pointed the way into the main hall. All of the seats were ripped out and stacked on the sides of the big room. Pappi found a place for the family on the floor.

"How long do we have to be here?" asked Tutti.

"I don't know, Tuttchen," said Mammi. "I don't know."

The Dutch Theater (Hollandsche Schouwburg) was renamed the Jewish Theater by the Nazis. The Lichtensterns stayed here for three days. This is where most of the Jews spent their last nights in Amsterdam before being transported to the camps. Tutti remembers sleeping on the floor and not receiving anything to eat or drink.

Oma (oh•mah): grandmother (German)

Opa (oh•pah): grandfather (German)

17

Westerbork
October 28, 1943

❧

The brakes screeched as the train jolted to a stop. Tutti had fallen asleep leaning against Mammi and almost fell out of her seat. Within seconds, the guards were opening the doors and yelling, "*Schnell, schnell, schnell!*" She couldn't move any faster. Her legs were cramped from sitting for days in the dark, stuffy theater and then sitting again on the train.

It was hard to believe that only days before, Pappi had been laughing joyfully about their new passport. That day had been so promising, but the next night they were sleeping on the floor of the Jewish Theater with the other Jews being sent to Westerbork. They had arrived at the theater by three o'clock, and had registered and been processed by evening. But it was three days before they were assigned to a transport—three days when there was nothing to eat but what Mammi had managed to stuff into their rucksacks, and nothing to do but grow more and more anxious about the future.

Now, coming down the steps of the train, Tutti saw a low building. It was gray, and above it the sky was also gray. The ground was muddy and it oozed into her shoes. She felt the damp chill of late October nightfall.

Tutti clutched Mammi's hand and hugged Roosje close. Looking up at her father, Tutti hoped for some sign that things would be okay. "Pappi, is this Westerbork?"

"Shh," whispered Margret, "let your father listen. The soldiers are giving directions." Then she bent down, looked Tutti in the eye, and said with determination, "It'll be all right. We will be okay."

Tutti cried a little but hurriedly rubbed her coat sleeve across her face so Robbie wouldn't see her tears and call her a baby. How could this be okay? They had hardly had anything to eat in four days. She was tired and hungry and thirsty. The people getting off the train all looked scared, and the guards were holding big guns and yelling.

Two of the guards shouted something and pushed Mammi and Tutti toward the mass of people. "You there— with the child. Get in line," they shouted at Pappi, who was holding Robbie while he juggled a suitcase and a rucksack.

The family lined up as they were told, and Tutti watched the people snake alongside the tracks over to the low gray building and then disappear inside. The guards stood close by, threatening anyone who sat down or strayed a few feet away. When Pappi finally got to the front of the line and they made their way into the building, Tutti saw a large room with rows of tables, where men and women sat with typewriters. All of them wore yellow stars, just like hers.

Then a space opened up at one of the tables and the clerk shouted, "Papers!"

Pappi stepped forward and handed the man a small leather billfold with his papers, including the Paraguayan passport.

"Are you Heinz Lichtenstern?"

"*Ja.*"

Westerbork's main street (called the Boulevard of Miseries)

"How old are you?"

"Thirty-six."

"And your wife? Her age?"

"Thirty-seven."

"How old are the children?"

"Five and eight."

"What is your profession?"

"I am a metals trader. I work for the Oxyde Company."

The man's harsh voice chilled Tutti, and she instinctively

moved closer to Mammi, who put her arm around her. She was scared because there was no smile from that man. No wink. Nothing to show her that he was aware that there were two hungry, tired, and confused children present. Robbie had his face buried in Mammi's coat.

As the man barked the questions, a woman with dark bags under her eyes sat beside him typing Pappi's answers. When the questions stopped, Pappi pointed at last to the passport. He straightened his shoulders, looked directly at the man, and proclaimed, "I am a citizen of Paraguay. The Third Reich is not at war with Paraguay. I should not be here."

The man looked up at Pappi and seemed to see him for the first time. "And I am a citizen of the Netherlands, and I should not be here either. Hold on to that passport. I can't do anything for you now, but it may help you later. We are told that there is a special camp where the Nazis send Jews who may be used in exchange for German prisoners of war, but here it does you no good. You are in the *Strafbaracke* number 67."

"*Strafbaracke? Prisoner* barracks? Aren't we all prisoners here?" asked Pappi.

"Yes and no. You didn't report when you were supposed to. Apparently, you were in hiding for some time. That means you and your family will be prisoners within the prison. I'm sorry. But there is nothing else I can do for you."

As they exited the building, Pappi was so preoccupied with this dismaying news—prisoners within the prison!— that he nearly walked into a guard standing beside an enormous pile of suitcases. "Jew!" yelled the guard, barring Pappi's path. "All bags must be left here!"

"We were told to bring these with us," Pappi said.

"All bags must be searched. They will be returned to you later."

Mammi and Pappi added their small suitcases to the pile and started toward the barracks with the children.

"Rucksacks, too!" shouted the guard. "And the doll!"

Mammi halted in the middle of taking off her rucksack. "It's just a child's doll," she said.

"We must search it. We'll return it later," he said adamantly.

Tutti looked pleadingly at her mother.

"Please, it's just a doll," repeated Mammi.

"Everything must be searched."

Tutti had no choice. She laid her doll gently on Mammi's suitcase. She never saw Roosje again.

Tutti's passport photo

schnell (shnehl): quickly (German)

18

Night Whispers

❧

That night, Tutti climbed down from the high third level of the bunk bed. She was careful not to wake Robbie, who slept on the middle level, as she made her way to curl up next to Mammi in the dark on the lower bunk. "Mammi, how long do we have to stay here?"

"I'm not sure, Tuttchen," she answered, gently rubbing Tutti's back.

"Where is Pappi?"

"He's in the men's barracks. It's right next door."

"I don't like it here. I don't like sleeping with all these people in one room."

Mammi didn't say anything. She simply rubbed Tutti's back and hummed.

"I couldn't sleep because of all the noise. I could hear at least five different snorers and six different coughers," said Tutti.

Mammi said, "I don't like this much either."

"My mattress is scratchy. The straw pokes through the cover," said Tutti.

"I know, Tuttchen. I'm sorry."

Somebody shushed them from the darkness.

Tutti and Mammi lay quietly, but Tutti couldn't sleep. "Mammi, I'm scared."

Mammi kept rubbing and humming. Then after a few minutes, she whispered, "There's one good thing about being here."

"Really? What?" asked Tutti.

"I didn't want to tell you until I was sure, but I will if you promise not to share this with Robbie yet."

"I promise! What's the good news, Mammi?" Tutti turned over to face her.

"I think Oma Flo and Opa Louis are here."

Tutti sat up, smiling. "Really?"

Another shush from someone nearby.

"I think so. We got a letter from them in August, and this is where it came from. I think Muttchen and Okkie are here, too!"

"Oh, Mammi, I miss them! How do we find out if they're here?"

"We'll figure it out in the morning. Now go to bed."

"Can I sleep here with you instead of up top?"

"Of course, Tuttchen." Mammi rubbed her back and Tutti lay in the dark, listening to the chorus of snoring, sniffling, and coughing—and hoping that she would soon see her grandparents again.

✣   ✣   ✣

In the morning, Tutti watched Mammi talk to everyone, even complete strangers. She asked questions. Who was here? How were they treated? When would their bags be returned? Then she took Tutti and Robbie outside to find Pappi.

Pappi had been gathering information as well. "Every Monday, they issue the list of people who will be sent East," he told Mammi, as they walked in the barracks yard. "It's not clear how those decisions are made, but I think—"

Barbed wire fence at Westerbork (2015)

Pappi suddenly stopped talking. He had heard some-thing . . . a familiar whistle: *Phweet, Phweet, Phweet, Phweet, Phweeeeeeee!*

"*Gott im Himmel!*" he exclaimed. Okkie was standing at the fence with Muttchen, Oma Flo, and Opa Louis.

Robbie ran, with Tutti just a few steps behind. As the children neared the fence, Mammi and Muttchen and Flo all yelled, "*Vorsichtig!*—be careful!"

Tutti grabbed Robbie before he could hurt himself on the barbed wire. She wanted to hug her grandparents, but of course the fence made that impossible. Still, it was the reunion they had all hoped for.

❧

Gott im Himmel (got ihm **him**•mehl): God in heaven (German)

vorsichtig (**fohr**•zish•tish): careful (German)

19

Scraps of Hope

November 1943

❧

Once Heinz had assured himself that his parents and his in-laws were all right, he turned his attention to getting his family out of the prisoner section of the camp.

He started by looking for Leopold Oberländer, who had been a manufacturer, and Josef Sax, who had run a steel company. He knew from Bobby Klopfer that both had been sent to Westerbork—and that Egbert had been trying to help them, as well.

Okkie found the two men, and before Heinz's first morning at Westerbork was over, he was speaking with them across the barbed wire fence.

"I thought my Paraguayan papers would keep us out of this godforsaken place," Heinz said when they asked whether the family's hiding place had been discovered. He couldn't bear to explain his mistake in leaving his friends' attic. "But that doesn't matter now. Tell me what's happening here. I see all those piles of scrap metal. There must be tons of it."

"*Ja,*" said Oberländer. "Egbert de Jong made arrangements for crashed planes to be brought here. The commandant, Gemmeker, set up a barracks for disassembling the planes and sorting the scrap."

"What's he doing with the scrap?" asked Heinz.

"He wants to turn this transit camp into a work camp," explained Sax. "He knows that there aren't many Jews left in the Netherlands. Once all the Jews are sent away, there won't be any need for a transit camp. If that happens, Gemmeker's out of a job. I think he's just as afraid of being sent East as we are! Turning this place into a work camp means he gets to avoid the front lines."

It was clear to Heinz that what Sax said was true. Gemmeker was benefiting from Egbert's plan, and Heinz had to find a way to turn it to his own advantage as well.

"What's Gemmeker doing with the scrap once it's sorted?" He wanted details, and he wanted them right away. He couldn't let his family stay in the prisoner barracks. More important, he had to find an angle that would save them, and he was sure that it would be hidden in the piles of twisted metal.

"When Oberländer and I arrived at the end of September," Sax said, "about 150 people were sorting the metals." With a ready pencil tucked behind his ear, Sax could work through any numbers to prove a point. "Last week, we had almost 600 people sorting the batteries, cables, and scrap. I'm sure we can put even more people to work at these jobs."

"So you have 600 people sorting metals. Then where does it go?" asked Heinz.

"We have been selling the scrap to smelters and processors in Amsterdam and The Hague. It brings in money for running the camp. More metal means more food."

"So why is there so much sorted metal in piles? Why haven't you sold it?"

"Lichtenstern, we're not in Amsterdam. This isn't your office at Oxyde," chided Oberländer. "These things take time."

Heinz's head was spinning. He knew this information was important. He could make himself useful in this scrap metal business and maybe, somehow, that would help his family. "Oberländer, Sax, you have to help me. You know I can move the metal. I know buyers all over the world."

"Lichtenstern, of course we'll include you in this. I was just saying to Sax last week that we needed someone who could help us move the metal out of the camp. I'm meeting with Gemmeker soon. I hope he will put me in charge of the whole metals sector. Then I'll tell him that I need you to go to Amsterdam to arrange for the sale of the metals. He already accepts Sax as our buyer. You'll be our seller. You're the one who will turn these piles of junk into cash for running the camp."

"Oberländer, you're a good man! Be sure to tell him that I know all the buyers. I have connections, and I'll use them."

❧ ❧ ❧

Two weeks later, Heinz paced along the barbed wire fence, waiting for Oberländer and Sax. When he made them out at a distance, he shouted, "Please tell me you have good news, Oberländer!"

"Lichtenstern, I've done it!"

"What happened?"

As an exuberant Oberländer explained it, he had convinced Gemmeker that business couldn't be conducted from the camp—that they needed more men in Amsterdam, where there were phones and where mail delivery was more reliable. He had also persuaded him to double or even triple the number of people sorting scrap in the camp. "Right now there are 600 people sorting, but I told him we could make it 1,000, maybe even 2,000. And with that increase, what we need is one person to buy the scrap and arrange for it to be brought to the camp, and then another person to sell it."

"And what did Gemmeker say to that?"

"He said yes. Gemmeker called Egbert de Jong, and de Jong backed me up, telling him that certainly the Dutch economy would be looking for the metals."

Egbert, thought Heinz, *you came through for me again!*

As matters now stood, Oberländer said that Heinz was considered an indispensable part of Westerbork's expanding metal operations. "Sax and you and I and several others are named in a letter from de Jong to the Department of Warfare and Munitions, saying that we are essential to the war industry."

"That's preposterous! We are *not* working for the Nazi war industry!" interrupted Heinz.

"No, of course we're not. But what can it hurt if the Nazis *think* we're helping them? This is how it'll work. Sax and you and I will be back in Amsterdam to handle buying and selling. Gemmeker told me that we'll have full access to the trams."

"What about our papers? The police will certainly stop us on the street. We'll be the only Jews left walking around with these damn yellow stars on our coats."

"No, we won't. We won't be wearing the stars at all. They're going to let us take the stars off. We'll have stamps on our papers giving us permission. Even the head of the *Sicherheitsdienst* won't be able to touch us!"

Heinz said nothing. He was still turning over the idea that he would in effect be helping the German military.

"Lichtenstern, don't you see the beauty of this? We will be free. Our families will be free. We'll bring the metal here and we'll have 2,000 Jews working. Those 2,000 Jews won't be sent East. They'll be able to stay here in the Netherlands!"

"But what about the metal going to the Third Reich?"

Oberländer lowered his voice. "Egbert has a plan for that, but you'll have to wait. We can't discuss that here. Please trust me."

The following week, on November 24, 1943, among the fourteen prisoners who were released from Westerbork were Heinz, Margret, Tutti, and Robbie Lichtenstern; Leopold and Lilli Oberländer; and Josef and Else Sax. They climbed into the back of a truck and were driven to Amsterdam, where they were free to resume their lives—so long as the men continued to buy and sell scrap metal.

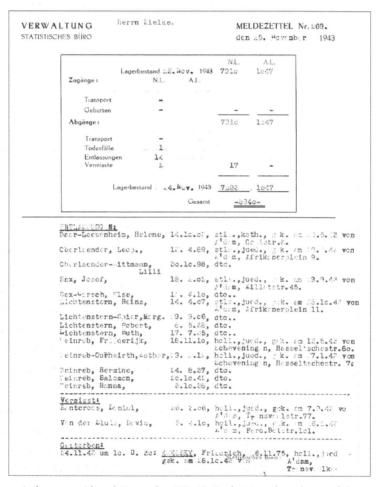

A document dated November 25, 1943, showing the release of the Oberländer, Sax, and Lichtenstern families on the previous day

20

Sabotage

November 24, 1943–February 9, 1944

❧

Heinz quickly found the family an apartment on Beethoven-straat. It wasn't home, but it was large and airy and far better than Afrikanerplein, with its tiny apartments on the east side of town. He understood the sorrowful reason for the glut of affordable apartments: the former tenants were Jews, whom the Nazis had arrested and shipped East.

That fact distressed him. But what could he do? The family needed a place to live. Margret worked her magic of making a home out of what she could find, and once again the family tried to establish its routines.

Heinz soon learned that Oxyde, the firm he had worked for and even temporarily directed, had been aryanized—stolen—by the Nazis. Of the original hundred employees, just twenty were still working; the remains of the company were now under Nazi control, and the office had been moved to the fourth floor of De Lairessestraat 6—by an unsettling coincidence, next door to the Lichtensterns' old house. More unsettling was the fact that an NSB man—a Nazi supporter—now lived there. Heinz wanted to spit on his old doorstep each time he passed. But instead, he threw his cigarette butt on the sidewalk and crushed it, leaving the trash for the new residents to clean up.

Heinz stayed in constant touch with Oberländer and Sax. Together, they secured enough scrap metal to keep the Jews in Westerbork busy. When they couldn't find metal on the open market, they went to the black market dealers. They always found enough metal to meet Gemmeker's quotas.

And all this time, Egbert was doing what he could to protect more Jews. One day, he called Gemmeker from Heinz's office. Sax and Oberländer were there, too.

"Commandant Gemmeker. I hope you are well. This is Egbert de Jong. I'm sorry to have to call with this news, but it seems that the metal isn't being sorted properly." Egbert went on to explain that some of the aluminum had been mixed in with the copper, and that the battery foils were caked with carbon. He paused and held the phone away from his ear. Heinz couldn't make out the words, but he could hear the worry in Gemmeker's voice.

Egbert continued. "Sir, please don't worry . . . I have a solution." He told Gemmeker to put more people at the sorting tables to check the work—and to appoint someone to watch each bin, just to make sure that nothing was put into the wrong one. He even listed names of several Westerbork inmates who would be good at those jobs—Heinz, Oberländer, and Sax's friends, whom they wanted to protect. "I will tell the smelters to have patience with the current shipment and promise them that the next batch will be sorted at a purer level . . . *Ja, ja, ja*. . . . *Heil Hitler.*"

Heinz shuddered upon hearing his friend say those awful words, but he had to admire his ingenuity and nerve.

"Egbert, I didn't know you had that much *chutzpah*," he said, after Egbert had hung up the phone. "That was pure genius. The smelters don't need the metal sorted so well."

Egbert sat back with his feet on the desk and his hands behind his head. "*Ja, I* know that . . . and *you* know that . . . but *Gemmeker* doesn't know that."

Sax was scribbling away on a scrap of paper. "You have just created work for another fifty Jews. That's fifty more who won't be sent to the East anytime soon."

But Heinz was torn. "Egbert, I'm still concerned about the metal helping those murderers. We may be keeping Jews from being sent East, but the Germans still get the metal for their airplanes and tanks."

"You're thinking about this the wrong way," Egbert said. "The sale of that scrap allows Gemmeker to buy food from the local farmers to feed the prisoners, to buy medicines for the camp hospital—and even costumes for Max Ehrlich's Westerbork Cabaret. Don't you see? He spends most of that money on Jews—the same Jews who are doing the work that doesn't really need to be done."

Egbert lit a cigarette. "Anyway, there's a part of the plan that I haven't explained to you yet. Those new people who will be making sure the sorting is done properly? Well, they'll actually be doing just the opposite."

"What in God's name are you talking about?"

"I want you to instruct them to put impurities in the barrels. Put aluminum in the steel. Add wire to the copper. Put gravel in the zinc. Do whatever you can to make the metals look sorted, but be sure they are full of impurities." Egbert's voice rose as he explained his plan. "I want their airplane wings to fall off and their submarines to be crushed when they dive too deep. We aren't giving them good metal. We are going to give the Germans the most defective metal we can get away with!"

A smile crossed Heinz's face. "The Jews stay in the Netherlands," he said. "The camp gets money for food and supplies. And the Nazis will build their airplanes and U-boats with junk. Now *this* is a plan I can live with!"

❧

chutzpah (<u>kh</u>**oots** • puh; *oo*, as in the *oo* in *took*): nerve (Yiddish)

21

Out of Luck

February 14–15, 1944

❧

"Oberländer!" Heinz shouted as he crossed the street toward his friend. He waited until he was closer to continue speaking. This was not a conversation to have in loud voices. "What happened? I received a letter this morning saying we are to report to the police station tomorrow."

"*Ja*, me too. Our luck has run out." Oberländer was looking down in disgust.

"But why? Do you think they know we were sabotaging the metal?" Heinz whispered.

"No. I don't think the Nazis have figured that out. They're too stupid. I think they just want to get all the Jews out of the Netherlands. Our scheme worked for a while, but we are out of time."

"What about Sax?"

"Sax, too." And then Oberländer dropped his voice even lower. "He said something about not reporting. He may go into hiding." Oberländer looked at Heinz. "What do you think? Shall we hide?" His eyes were imploring his friend for advice. For once, Oberländer did not have a plan.

Heinz didn't hesitate for a moment. "No. My parents and Margret's parents are at Westerbork. If I don't report—"

OT-157

15.

BdS.
IV B 4 e - B.Nr.10324/44.   Den Haag, den 10.Februar 1944.

04558

3.... 6 1/ FEB 1944

1.) Bernschreiben:

An die
Zentralstelle für jüdische Auswanderung
zu Hd. von SS-Hauptsturmführer aus der Fünten,

A m s t e r d a m .

Betrifft: Jüdische Metallaufkäufer in den Niederlanden.

Lt. Erlass des RSHA. - IV B 4 a - 3 - 597/43 g (370)
sind die aus dem Lager Westerbork entlassenen und als
Metallaufkäufer eingesetzten Juden
    Heinz Lichtenstern, geb.14.4.1907,
    I. Sachs, geb. 18.2.1902, und
    Leopold Israel Oberländer, geb.14.4.1889,
    mit ihren Familien ,
mit Rücksicht auf die unverzügliche völlige Entjudung
der Niederlande sofort wieder festzunehmen und in das
Lager Westerbork zurückzuführen. Die Juden sind für die
Umsiedlung nach Theresienstadt vorgesehen. Es besteht
die Möglichkeit, dass die Juden zur Ausübung ihrer
Tätigkeit sich z. Zt. ausserhalb Amsterdams befinden.

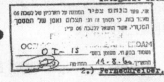

BdS.,Den Haag - IV B 4 e - B.Nr.10324/44.
    Im Auftrage:
    gez. Z o e p f .
    SS-Sturmbannführer.

2.) Fernschreiber.

3.) I C austragen und zurück an IV B 4 e (Slottke).

13/31.7.

This February 10, 1944, order to arrest Lichtenstern, Sax (in the document above, his name is misspelled as Sachs), and Oberländer and their families was placed into evidence on August 11, 1960, at the Adolph Eichmann trial in Israel, which is why there is a stamp near the bottom with words in Hebrew.

98

He shook his head, unable to finish the thought out loud. "I have to go. Besides, I tried hiding. My nerves were terrible. Every noise made me jump. I can't handle that again."

"I need to discuss things with Lilli," Oberländer said, beginning to walk away.

"Will I see you tomorrow on Euterpestraat?" Heinz called.

Oberländer turned back and shrugged his shoulders without saying a word. Then he shuffled on toward his apartment to talk with his wife about the impossible choice they had to make.

❧   ❧   ❧

The next day, Oberländer and Lichtenstern reported with their families as ordered. Sax and his wife didn't show up.

Heinz worried about this turn of events. *What if Oberländer and I are punished because of Sax's decision? And even if we aren't, will Oberländer and I be able to keep the metalworks scheme going and our families at Westerbork?*

There were no longer enough Jews left in Amsterdam for the Nazis to bother with a train, so the small group was transported by truck. *We must succeed. We must make it work.* Heinz's thoughts went round and round.

On the bumpy ride back, Robbie got motion sickness and vomited. Margret put her arm around him and sang to him, though in the open truck, it was hard to hear anything, and talking was nearly impossible. Tutti sat on the other side of her mother, watching through the rails of the truck as the city turned to farmland, and the countryside turned to wasteland.

By the time they reached the camp gates, Tutti was freezing and her ears were ringing, but at least Robbie's face looked less green as he climbed out of the truck. This time there was no line for registration, as only a few families were being processed. They stood in front of one of the tables, and Heinz began to mechanically answer the questions. He said nothing about the passport. He already knew it wouldn't do any good.

Heinz thought of the terrible *Strafbaracke* with the rows and rows of triple bunks and no privacy. He made eye contact with Margret as they stood with their children. She returned his gaze with sadness. He knew she didn't blame him, but he also knew she was upset about being back in this purgatory. Heinz was having a silent conversation with Margret. He furrowed his brow and mouthed, "I'm so sorry." As he looked at his wife, he saw her expression change before his eyes. The corners of her mouth curved upwards, her eyes opened a bit wider, and even her cheeks regained some color. She turned to the children and said in a hopeful voice, "*Kinder*, remember, your grandparents are here."

The official behind the table asked more questions, Heinz and Margret answered, and the typist plucked away at her keys with short bursts of *rat-a-tat-tat*. When the clerk was done typing, she handed a stiff paper to Heinz and said, "Barracks 42."

The four Lichtensterns picked up their bags and started walking toward the *Strafbaracke*.

Oberländer stopped them. "Lichtenstern, where are you going?"

"To the barracks. I want to get Margret and the children settled," Heinz answered despondently.

"Why are you going that way?"

"I'm going to the barracks—over in the *strafe* section."

"Lichtenstern, didn't you hear what they told you? You are in barracks number 42. We are nearby in number 44."

"So?" Heinz was confused.

"Lichtenstern, for God's sake, read the ID card they gave you."

Heinz looked at the card for the first time. It had his name and birthdate. It listed his occupation as a salesman and his last known address in Amsterdam. It said the date and that he would be in group DB 12. That was the metal works. And then at the bottom of the card in the section for remarks it said *Stammliste*.

Heinz's Westerbork identification card

Margret was growing impatient. "Well, what does it say?" she asked as she took the card out of his hand. "*Stammliste!* Heinz, we're on the *Stammliste*—the privileged list." She dropped her bag and hugged her husband.

He hugged her back, but he wasn't convinced that this was going to mean anything. "What could be a privilege in a place like this?" he whispered.

"Let's find out," said Margret as she headed in the direction in which Oberländer was pointing.

The special privileges were apparent immediately when they arrived at their assigned barracks. The long, low building had several doors and windows, and their single room, 9 feet by 12 feet, housed two cots, a table, and three chairs.

Heinz finally smiled. This would be much more tolerable than the prisoner barracks.

Tutti and Robbie each rushed to claim a bed of their own. Margret sighed. "Tutti, Robbie, you two will be sharing this bed. Pappi and I will share the other." Margret's voice was sympathetic, yet stern enough that the children knew not to argue.

Within an hour of the family's second Westerbork arrival, eight people were all crowded into the little room that was now home. They were hugging and crying and laughing, relieved to be safely together again after twelve weeks—even in a place like this. Opa Louis held Robbie on his lap, Muttchen marveled at how much Tutti had grown, Margret and Oma Flo held each other, and Heinz shared a cigarette with his father.

22

The List

February 25, 1944

❧

On Monday afternoon, just days after their return to Westerbork, Tutti noticed that all the adults were tense and preoccupied and seemed to have little time for her. "Mammi, what's the list?" she asked at bedtime.

"What have you heard about a list?" asked Mammi.

"Not much. I just kept hearing people talk about the list today, and they were upset when they talked about it. What is it a list of?"

"Tuttchen, it's hard to explain."

"But why does it make people unhappy? Mammi, please tell me."

"All right, Tutti." Mammi sighed and rubbed her neck. Tutti could tell that she was thinking. Finally she said, "Robbie, you should listen, too. You know that the Germans sent us here to Westerbork. Well, the Germans have other camps. Sometimes they send people from one camp to another, but before they do that, they put those people on a list. They announce the list on Monday night, and then those people leave on the train on Tuesday."

"Are we on the list, Mammi?" Robbie asked.

"No. No, we're not on the list. As a matter of fact, there was no list today. People were worried, but then the list was never posted. We can stay right here. You two go to sleep now. I'll see you in the morning. *Schlaf gut.*"

The next two days were quiet. Tutti discovered that some of the friends she had made back in November were still here, though most were not, and she realized, sadly, that *they* had been put on the list. She and Robbie joined the other children in their games and went to a few classes led by prisoners who had been teachers before the war. Soon it was easy to forget that they had ever left the camp. Then on Thursday afternoon, when Tutti came into the family's room to get out of the biting wind, she saw that Mammi's eyes were red.

"What is it, Mammi? Is everything okay?"

"Tutti, everything's fine." Margret avoided eye contact with her daughter.

"But Mammi, you look so sad," insisted Tutti.

"I'm all right. It's . . . it's . . . we have to say goodbye to your grandparents again."

"Opa Louis and Oma Flo? Or Okkie and Muttchen?"

"All of them. They're all on the list."

"I thought there wasn't a list this week."

"Oh, Tuttchen, that's what we thought. But they didn't skip the list this week—it was just late." Tutti heard the catch in Mammi's voice. She was struggling not to cry.

"Where are they going?"

"To Theresienstadt."

"Where's that?"

"It's in Czechoslovakia," answered Mammi.

"Is it far away? Can we visit them there?" There had to be something that would make Mammi feel better.

"No, I'm afraid we can't visit them." Mammi was having trouble getting the words out.

Tutti turned away in distress. Her mother's sorrow was unbearable. "At least can we go with them to the train to wave goodbye?" she asked.

"Yes, Tuttchen. That's a wonderful idea," Mammi said. "I'll wake you up when it's time."

The next morning, the family accompanied the four grandparents to the boarding area. Only ten days before, they had all embraced with smiles on their faces. Now they were embracing again, but this time with tears in their eyes.

"Oma Flo, what's it like in Theresienstadt?" Tutti asked, as she hugged her grandmother goodbye.

"The Germans told us it's a very nice place, Tuttchen. It's a camp for older people and it's a bit like a vacation spa. Don't worry about us. We'll see each other again soon."

Tutti and Robbie held hands while they waved goodbye to their grandparents. A vacation spa didn't sound bad. Maybe Mammi didn't know about that. She would tell her as soon as the train was out of sight.

❧

schlaf gut (shlahf **goot**): sleep well (German)

Theresienstadt (teh•**ray**•zee•uhn•**shtaht**): A fortress in German-controlled Czechoslovakia used by the Nazis as a transit/ghetto-labor camp (see Historical Notes) (German)

25.2.44

351.	Kesnig	Eliazer	15. 1.02	Buecherrevisor
352.	Kesnig-Horn	Rachel	9. 4.09	Pflegerin
353.	Kirschstein	Ilse J.	2. 3.24	Naeherin
354.	Kisch	Herman	15. 6.82	Kaufmann
355.	Kisch-Philips	Sara	1. 5.93	Ohne
356.	Koe	Salomon	5. 1.74	Diamantschleifer
357.	Koekoek	Barend	13. 7.11	Angestellter
358.	Koekoek-Michaels	Goderta	28. 9.11	Lehrerin
359.	Koekoek	Henri	11. 4.39	Ohne
360.	Koekoek	Henriette	16. 4.08	Pflegerin
361.	Kokoskij-v.Kollem	Hanna	28. 8.04	Korrespondentin
362.	Kooker	Godfroid	15. 3.04	Friseur
363.	Kool-Bronkhorst	Sara	29. 1.91	Kontoristin
364.	Krakauer	Herbert	12.10.27	Kontoristin
365.	Krant-Cohen	Reina	2. 4.04	Mantelnaeherin
366.	Krant	Betje	5. 8.31	Ohne
367.	Kretschner-Roth	Hulda	29. 5.70	Ohne
368.	Kuiper	Ben	12.11.74	Kaufmann
369.	Kuijt	Mejjer	22.12.06	Kaufmann
370.	Kuijt-Leeser	Hendrika	21. 4.07	Naeherin
371.	Kujt	Michel	28. 6.30	Ohne
372.	Kuijt	Rebecca	8. 6.35	Ohne
373.	Kujt	Mozes	10. 3.00	Angestellter
374.	Kut-Verdoner	Sientje	10. 9.99	Ohne
375.	Kwieser	Henri	3.1. 03	Kontorist
376.	Kwieser-Cohen	Mirjam	28. 5.08	Ohne
377.	Kwieser	Hettij	15. 9.32	Ohne
378.	Lange	Heinr.ch	19. 9.93	Versicherungsagent
379.	Lange-Schragenheim	Ilse	17. 6.03	Ohne
380.	Lange	Johanna	22. 3.32	Ohne
381.	de Leeuw	Max	23. 6.16	Pfleger
382.	Leon	Clara	8. 6.04	Naeherin
383.	de Leon	Georgine	10. 1.02	Pflegerin
384.	Leon	Jacob	25. 2.00	Buchhaendler
385.	Leon	Marianne	10. 1.07	Kontoristin
386.	de Leon	Wilhelmina	30.10.98	Pflegerin
387.	Lewt Dr.	Max	19. 2.86	Ingenieur
388.	Lichtenstern.Caro	Jennij	10.12.77	Beamtin
389.	Lichtenstern	Oscar	3.12.75	Beamter
390.	Lobatto	August	22. 5.80	Kaufmann
391.	Lobatto	Clara	23. 2.70	Ohne
392.	Lobatto	Louise	6.12.73	Pianolehrerin
393.	Lobatto-van Gelder	Rebecca	13. 3.95	Ohne
394.	Loeb-Majjer	Dina	12. 7.94	Disetassistentin
395.	Loeb	Ilse	30. 1.20	Laborantin
396.	Lowenthal	Artur	27. 9.06	Kaufmann
397.	Loewenthal	Fedor	24. 9.76	Ohne
398.	Lowenthal-Kaufmann	Emma	25. 2.79	Ohne
399.	Loewenthal gesch. Rademacher	Luise	9. 4.03	Ohne
400.	Lewtj	Ilse	8. .7.17	Hausangestellte

Two pages of the transport list from February 25, 1944,
with Jenny Lichtenstern (#388), Oscar Lichtenstern (#389),
Flora Spier (#656), and Louis Spier (#657).

651 de Sola	Hilda	2o.5.o5	ohne
652 de Souza (Henriques)	Rachel	13.4.82	ohne
653 de Souza	Samuel	23.11.83	Bankdirektor
654 Speijer	Auguste	15.1.o3	Kontoristin
655 Speyer- Moddel	martha	23.2.79	ohne
656 Spier-Lijon	Flora	19.2.82	Näherin
657 Spier	Louis	9.11.73	Lederfabrikant
658 Spinoza Catella-Jessurun	Betty	9.1o.18	Pflegerin
659 Spinoza-Catella-Jewsurun	Rachel	12.12.81.	Pflegerin
66o Spinaza-Catella-Jessurun	Rebecca	13.9.8o	Lehrerin
661 Swaab	Juda	18.2.o4	Zahnarzt
662 Swaab-Marchand	Hendrika	1o.11.o4	ohne
663 Wittelshöfer	Stefanie	1.5.29	Schülerin
664 Schaefer	Walter	16.11.93	Dentist
665 Scheiberg	Sally G.	13.1o.93	Häutehändler
666 Scheiberg-v. Esso	Vera	13.8.o6	ohne
667 Scheiberg	Dorothea	27.12.3o	ohne
668 Schoenthal	Max	24.12.88	Strumpfreperateur
669 Schoenthal-Zaum	Rachel	12.2.86	ohne
67c schut	Frank	16.1o.o4	Beamter
671Schwab	Hannah	17.1o.23	Näherin
672 Stern	Herman	17.12.93	Chemiker
673 Stibbe	Cate	14.4.1o	Stenotypistin
674 Stibbe	Inge	27.12.36	ohne
675 Stoeckl-Blumenfeld	Ilonka	26.12.o7	ohne
676 Stokvis-Montezinos	Lea	5.7.72	ohne
677Strox	Laja	1o.4.o6	Schneiderin
678 Stuiver	Alexander	21.3.o5	Kaufmann rin
679 Stuiver -Balle	Sara	8.6.o7	Maschinenstrickerin
68o Stuiver	Isaac	19.1o.3o	ohne
681 Styckin	Abram	9.6.95	Uhrmacher
682 Theeboom	Louise	8.7.2o	Diamantschneider
683 Theeboom	Sientje	1.2.18	Kontoristin er
684 Teixeira de Mattos	Freerk	2.8.17	Maschinentechnik
685 Teixeira de Mattos	Hettyöx	15.1o.15	Pflegerin
686 Teixeira de Mattos	Jacob	27.3.87	Kontorist
687 Teixeira de Mattos-Vas Nunes, Rebecca		11.1.91	ohne
688 Teixeira de Mattos	Joseph	13.12.85	Rektor
689 Teixeira de Mattos-Namias	Judith	3o.7.68	ohne
69o Teixeira de Mattos	Rachel	6.1o.o3	Näherin
691 Teixeira de Mattos	Raphael	1o.1.91	Bücherrevisor
692 Teixeira de Mattos-Italie	Dina	27.8.93	ohne
693 Teixeira de Mattos	Erika	31.12.3o	ohne
694 Teixeira de Mattos	Samuel	13.6.8o	ohne
695 Teixeira de Mattos	Selly	19.3.85	Krankenpflegerin
696 Teppich	Hellmut. B.	12.3.23	Landarbeiter
697 de Torres	David	1.3.83	Buchhalter
698 de Torres -Rodrigues-Pereira, Margaretha		2.11.86	ohne
699 Trompetter	Maurita	2o.5.79	Administrateur
7ooTrompetter-Plesseman	Marianna	7.3.86	ohne

23

Barbed Wire

❧

For Tutti, one of the worst things about being at Westerbork was the food, which was prepared for inmates by a central kitchen for distribution to the barracks. The cooks used the poorest ingredients, and the portions were often far too small. But Mammi stuck to her routine, and called the children in for meals as if she had prepared the food herself on her own stove in Amsterdam.

"Tutti, it's time for dinner," she said one day. "Can you find Robbie and tell him to come home?"

When the children returned, Robbie was grinning. "Mammi, I have a surprise." He pulled half a loaf of bread out from under his shirt.

"Where did this come from?" Mammi asked sharply.

"I don't know," he said sheepishly.

"Robbie?"

"Well, well, you see—" He hesitated.

"Robbie!"

"Well, these two men were talking, arguing, really. I don't know what they were arguing about, but they were pointing at each other and yelling and the bread was on the table. They weren't paying any attention to the bread, and I didn't think they would miss it, so when another man started yelling at the first two men, I grabbed the bread and ran."

"Robbie!" Mammi scolded.

"But we need it! They were just letting it sit there on the table. Anyway, there are birds all over the fields. If I hadn't taken the bread, I bet a whole flock of them would have swooped down and eaten it. You always say not to waste food."

"Never mind. Please put the bread on the table and sit down. Tutti, you too."

Mammi gave the pot one last stir and ladled the thin broth into the four bowls.

Tutti picked up her spoon and looked at the soup. She wished it smelled better, but as usual there was a faint odor of something rotten in it. She wished it looked better, but it was the same gray watery liquid as every night. Above all, she wished it tasted better. She was very hungry, but she did not want to eat it.

"Mammi—" Tutti began. She didn't like to whine, but it was hard to stop herself. "Mammi, I don't like this. Why do we have the same thing every day?"

"It's all we have," Mammi said matter-of-factly.

"I wish we had a meat bone or fresh vegetables." Tutti remembered the soup her mother used to make at home. It would simmer all day, and it would be full of turnips and parsley and potatoes. When Mammi put in a meat bone, the broth would become brown and thick, and the heavenly smell would waft through the whole house. She inspected the thin broth again. All it had in it was a few peapods with their tough strings.

"I know you don't like the soup, Tuttchen, but there are vitamins in it," said Pappi, as Mammi divided the bread, giving the largest pieces to the children.

Tutti decided to eat the strings little by little, between spoonfuls of broth. That way, she didn't have to deal with them all at once. It was difficult to chew them well enough to swallow easily.

"Robbie, please keep your mouth closed when you chew," said Mammi.

"I can't. The strings are all wiry." He chomped with exaggerated motions as he pushed the tough pods around his bowl.

"Robbie, use your spoon. Get those filthy fingers out of your bowl," Pappi said in irritation. They all ate quietly for a few minutes.

Robbie interrupted the silence. "Tutti, look, I have barbed wire in the middle of my bowl."

"What do you mean? Nobody cooks with wire," insisted Tutti.

"The Germans do. The peapod strings. They're just like wire. I'm going to start calling this *prikkeldraad soep*." Robbie was pointing at the fence he had made in the middle of his bowl.

"It does feel like we're biting wires. *Prikkeldraad soep*," Tutti giggled.

"Shush, *Kinder*," Pappi reproached them wearily. "It isn't barbed wire. Please . . . just eat. And stop playing with your soup."

Mammi looked at Pappi and smiled to lighten his mood. "Barbed wire soup. It really isn't such a bad name."

❧

prikkeldraad soep (prih•kehl•draht soop): barbed wire soup (Dutch)

24

Compromised

June 1944

᠅

"Goodbye, Tuttchen. *Auf Wiedersehen*, Robbie. I'll see you in three days." The children had been playing in the dirt, but they looked up when Pappi, wearing his hat and coat, came outside with Mammi. Heinz ruffled Robbie's hair and gave Tutti a hug.

"Where are you going?" asked Robbie.

"I'm going to work in Amsterdam," Pappi answered. "I have a work pass from Commandant Gemmeker. I'm going to sell the metal that the workers here have been sorting."

"Do you have to carry those big piles of metal with you to the city?" asked Robbie.

Heinz smiled and let out a little laugh. "No, no, Robbie. I just talk to the people who might want it, we make a deal, and then they will send a truck for it."

"So does Commandant Gemmeker pay you, Pappi?" asked Tutti.

Heinz sighed a little uncomfortably. The conversation was about to become more complicated. "No, Tutti. He doesn't pay me. Westerbork has to make money so that the camp can buy food to feed all of us here. I know you don't like the food very much, but if I don't help sell the metal, the food will be even worse, and there will be less of it, too."

"Pappi," Robbie said, "when you sell the metal, you should make a good deal, and then maybe the food will be better. Maybe we could have pancakes! Maybe even pancakes with chocolate!" Robbie licked his lips.

"Oh, Robbie—no pancakes and certainly no chocolate. But at least we will have soup and bread."

"Soup and bread!" Tutti exclaimed. "It seems like there's a lot more metal around here than just enough for peapods."

Heinz was in a hurry—and the conversation was getting awkward. But he decided to be as straightforward as possible. "Well, you're right. The Germans take some of the money from the metal sales for themselves. And they don't sell all of the metal. They use some of it, too."

"So you're helping the Germans?" Tutti looked at her father in dismay.

How was he going to explain this? He'd made this compromise because there seemed to be no other choice, but compromises were hard for children to understand. "Unfortunately, yes. In order to help all of us here in the camp, I have to help the Germans, too."

"I don't like it, Pappi. I don't like you working for the Germans," cried Robbie. He picked up a stone and threw it hard into a nearby puddle.

"Oh, Robbie, you splashed mud all over my shoes!" Tutti yelled.

"*Kinder*, please stop fighting." Heinz's voice was weary more than angry. "Margret, I've got to leave now. Maybe you can explain this better than I can."

After Heinz had gone, Margret did her best. "Pappi helps the Germans a little so he can help us—all of us at this camp—a lot. You know how the trains come and take people to other camps?"

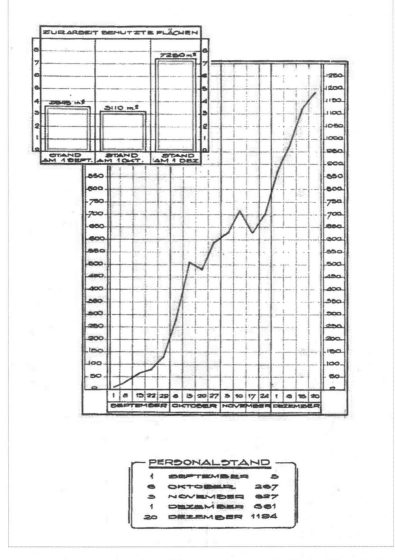

A graph showing the number of Jews sorting metal in 1943 at Westerbork: On September 1, 1943, there were five Jews sorting metals. On December 20, 1943, after Oberländer, Sax, and Lichtenstern became involved in the metals operation, that number increased to 1,194.

"Like Oma Flo and Opa Louis and Muttchen and Okkie?" asked Tutti.

"Yes, like your grandparents. Well, those camps are not as nice as this one, and they're not in the Netherlands. You see, if your father can keep the Germans satisfied with the metal sorting, then more people will be able to stay here and won't be sent to those other camps. He's trying to help everyone at Westerbork."

The children listened but didn't respond. Margret decided to change the subject.

"Your father said he would try to bring back extra food for us from Amsterdam—maybe some milk and butter this time. Now run along and play nicely. I have to report to work at the laundry."

❧

auf Wiedersehen (owf **vee**•dehr•zehn): goodbye (German)

25

A Brave Choice

❧

It was the final day of Heinz's trip to Amsterdam. The tower clock on the Royal Palace showed ten minutes past three. With little more than twenty minutes to catch his train, Heinz made a decision. Like so many other choices he had made in the past few years, this one was potentially a matter of life and death. He glanced at the clock high above Dam Square one more time and scurried into the store. Passing the mostly empty display cases, he walked to the children's shelf with toy cars, jump ropes, and marbles. Looking into the eyes of a doll, he took a deep breath and considered what he was about to do.

"We have only one doll left, I'm afraid," said the shopkeeper. "It's quite plain, but it would make a nice companion for a little girl. Do you have a daughter?"

"Ja," Heinz answered in Dutch.

"How old is she?" asked the clerk.

"Her birthday is next week. She'll be nine."

The chatty clerk dropped her smile and said coldly, "Shall I wrap it for you?"

"Ja, alstublieft." He answered "yes, please" in Dutch, but he couldn't hide his German accent, and he knew the clerk was put off by it. But how could Heinz explain himself? He was a starless, stateless Jew with a German accent carrying a Paraguayan passport on a work pass from a concentration camp.

Heinz paid for the doll, which the clerk had wrapped in several sheets of paper, and tucked the bundle under his arm like a Frenchman carrying a baguette. He looked again at the clock—3:15. He walked as fast as he could without actually running to Amsterdam Centraal. The place was abuzz with the bustle of many people, and Heinz zigzagged through the crowd. He found the men's room and then locked the door to the stall and sat down. Balancing the doll on his lap, he got to work with the precision of a surgeon. Once finished with the task, he held the doll in front of him to study his handiwork. *Good as new,* he thought, wrapping it back up and stuffing it into his rucksack.

He heard an announcement over the din in the station as he left the men's room—the final call for his train. Heinz headed to the platform, picking up speed as he went. His stride got longer, his breath louder, and then, just a moment after he stepped inside, the door closed behind him and the train lurched forward.

He stood in the third-class car, leaning against the wall for support, and felt his heart pounding. The conductor was making his way down the aisle, and when he asked for Heinz's identification papers and his ticket, Heinz held his breath as he handed them over. The conductor inspected both, stamped the ticket, and moved on to someone else. Only then did the thumping of Heinz's heart slow down.

When he got back to the camp, Margret gave Heinz a huge hug. "How was Amsterdam?"

Tutti and Robbie both climbed onto his lap, competing for the best spot.

"*Alles gut, Kinder!* I have cans of milk, and a little butter, and some other things. Here, Margret, you should take this."

Heinz tried to push his rucksack toward her, but it was difficult to manage with both children on his lap.

"Pappi, did you bring me anything?" asked Robbie.

"And what about me?" asked Tutti.

"*Kinder*, it wasn't a shopping trip or a vacation. It was work. I was lucky to find the milk and the butter."

"Tell us about Amsterdam," said Tutti, as Margret took the rucksack and rifled through it. When she looked at Heinz questioningly, he winked and motioned to her to put it away.

"Pappi will tell you about it later," Margret said. "Right now, he needs to rest for a few minutes. Why don't you go outside and play?"

Tutti knew what *that* meant: it meant, "Pappi and I need to have a private conversation." She sighed, took Robbie's hand, and led him outside.

❧

ja, alstublieft (yah, ahls•tew•**bleeft**): yes, please (Dutch)

26

Surprise Party

July 17, 1944

❧

One unusually dry, sunny day in July, Tutti sat on the pathway to the barracks with Klaus Walbaum and Ursula Heilbut. They were drawing in the dried mud with small sticks.

"Tutti!" Robbie came running around the corner and stopped right in front of her.

"Robbie, move. You're on my picture."

Robbie stood smiling at his sister, while Klaus, Ursula, and Tutti all glared at him.

"Robbie, move!" Tutti stood up and pushed him.

"Mammi said you have to come home right now," said Robbie.

"I don't believe you. Why are you smiling like that?" Tutti worried that her little brother knew she had a crush on Klaus. She pushed him again to make sure he was clear of her drawing and sat down. "Ugh, now my drawing is ruined. I have to start over."

As Tutti moved over to a new spot to draw on, Robbie tried again. "Mammi said you have to come home right now!" This time his voice was more urgent.

"Is something wrong?" Tutti asked as she stood to wipe the dried mud off her bottom.

"No, it's good. Come on." Robbie grabbed her hand and pulled her toward the barracks.

When Tutti arrived, she couldn't believe her eyes. There was a cake on the table. "Happy birthday!" her parents chimed in unison.

Tutti was astonished. "Mammi, how did you make a cake?"

"You know your mother can make wonderful things out of nothing," said Pappi, with a loving look at his wife.

"Tutti, it isn't a cake like we would have at home. It's made out of grated potatoes," Mammi explained.

Tutti's heart sank a little, and the buttery vanilla sponge cake she had briefly imagined now disappeared from her head. But she hugged her mother anyway. "Oh, Mammi, thank you! I didn't even remember that today was my birthday."

The family sat down, and Mammi carefully cut the potato cake into four pieces. Tutti knew that it wasn't real cake, but she didn't care. It was her birthday, and her mother had made her something special, and they were celebrating.

Robbie took a big bite and spit the mouthful back onto his plate. "This isn't cake," he said indignantly.

"I told you. It's potatoes. I *shaped* it like a cake," explained Mammi.

"But I thought we were having a *real* cake," whined Robbie.

"We are, Robbie. It's potato cake. And *I* like it!" Tutti was not going to let her little brother ruin her birthday.

"But it tastes—" Robbie stopped in mid-sentence as Pappi glared at him.

Pappi finished his serving with a quick three bites and then jumped up and pulled a bundle wrapped in brown paper from under the bed. "Tutti, here's a present for you. Happy birthday!"

Tutti's face lit up. "Really, Pappi? What is it?"

"Open it and you'll see," he said.

Tutti tore open the papers and squealed with delight at the sight of the most beautiful doll she had ever seen. Her eyes were a shiny brown. Her dress, crisp and pressed, was the same blue as the sky on a perfect summer day. She had a matching kerchief on her head and a lock of brown hair forming a curl on her forehead. "Pappi, I love her! She's so pretty! Where did she come from?"

"On my last trip to Amsterdam, I was able to spend a few minutes shopping. As soon as I saw her, I knew that this doll had to come back with me for your birthday."

"Oh, Pappi, thank you!" Tutti threw herself into her father's arms. "Can I show Ursula?"

Tutti's Popje (2015)

"Of course you can," Mammi said. "But it's getting late. Please come back soon."

"Ursula!" Tutti called as she ran out the door. "Look! Look what Pappi gave me for my birthday! Look at my beautiful *popje!*" And right then she decided that Popje—Dolly—would be her name.

🌱

popje (pop•yah): dolly (Dutch)

120

27

The Visitor

❖

"Margret, please do something about the noise. I need to study these numbers," Heinz said in frustration.

Margret sat on the bed between the rambunctious children. She took Robbie's feet and put them on her lap. "Do you know the story of the ten little mice?" she asked, gently pinching one of Robbie's toes.

Heinz watched with relief as the children settled down for a story. They didn't understand this life or the danger they were in if he didn't produce enough metal. The latest plan he'd made with Oberländer and de Jong—reclaiming part of the metal from the smelters and pretending it was new scrap—was not sustainable in the long term, and the possibility of getting caught kept him awake at night. He needed to increase production—and soon. If not, it was his children who would suffer.

". . . and so the last little mouse was happy in her little mouse bed with her five mouse brothers and four mouse sisters, and they all went to sleep." Margret finished the story and gave both children a squeeze, tucked them under the blanket on either end of the bed, and kissed them both on the forehead. "*Gute Nacht. Schlaf gut, meine Kinder.*" She pulled the sheet that substituted as a wall to section off the bed from the rest of the room and went to sit with Heinz.

Behind the thin sheet, Tutti and Robbie were beginning their nightly battle of kicking and blanket-pulling. Heinz could hear every grunt and every "ouch!" He tried to ignore their squabbling and told himself that they would soon give up and fall asleep. He was scheduled to go to The Hague again, and Margret would have a long day tomorrow at the laundry. He knew that she worried whenever he left camp.

"Good evening, Herr Lichtenstern."

Heinz started, looked up from his numbers, and saw Commandant Gemmeker standing in the doorway. He rose and opened his mouth to say something, but no words came out.

"Commandant Gemmeker, please, sit down," Margret said. If she was surprised, she didn't show it. Gemmeker sat in one of the plain wooden chairs, and Heinz returned to his seat across the table.

There was a brief moment when no one said anything, and in the silence, Heinz realized that Robbie and Tutti had ceased their fighting.

Then Gemmeker said, "Herr Lichtenstern, how are you?" He actually sounded as if he cared.

"We're well," Heinz said. "Or, as well as can be expected."

"And how is the metal sorting going? I was hoping that we would have more copper to send to Berlin this week."

Heinz swallowed. Did Gemmeker know what he and Oberländer had set up? "They sort what they have." He hoped his voice sounded normal, calm. "Right now, they only have batteries to work with. I'm scheduled to go to The Hague tomorrow. I'll find more scrap and will set up some advanced sales as well. The laborers are at it all day. You see how they work. Maybe if we had a few more men—"

The commandant interrupted him. "The trip to The Hague is cancelled. Berlin has ordered the camp to scale down."

"Wh— what does that mean?" stammered Heinz. He was confused. He had hoped that he and his family could stay in the Netherlands for the rest of the war. Westerbork wasn't luxury, but they were alive. If they were sent to the East, it could mean greater hardship and suffering—or worse.

"There will be only a few more transports and you and your family will need to be on one of them. I thought you might want some time to prepare." Then Gemmeker stood, tipped his hat in Margret's direction, and left the room without closing the door.

Margret and Heinz stared at each other in silence for several minutes. Margret pulled a handkerchief out of her sleeve and blew her nose into it. Then she slowly shut the door and whispered, "I guess we'd better pack."

Herr (hehr): Mr. (German)

Gute Nacht. Schlaf gut, meine Kinder (goo•tuh nah<u>kht</u>; shlahf **goot, mine**•uh **kihn**•dehr): Good night. Sleep well, my children. (German)

28

Popje's Secret

❧

The next evening, Pappi sat with Tutti on the bed that she shared with Robbie and spoke to her in a very serious voice. "Tutti, I need to talk with you about something important."

They were alone. After dinner, Mammi had told Robbie that she wanted to take a walk with him—and now Pappi wanted to talk to her. What was he going to say? Had she done something wrong? Or were they being sent East?

Pappi said, "Let me have Popje for a minute. I want to show you something about her."

Popje? Now Tutti was confused. She handed her doll to Pappi, who held her gently on his lap. "Tutti, you see here? Her head is a bit loose," he said, tapping her chin. "It isn't going to fall off, but it's wobbly."

"How did that happen? I've been so careful with her! I promise I'll take better care of her, Pappi. Really, I will."

Pappi smiled. "I'm not angry with you, Tuttchen. It isn't your fault. Actually, I wanted to tell you that *I* did it."

Tutti was more confused than ever. "But why, Pappi? Why would you do that?"

"Well, I had to so I could put something inside. Tutti, you know we have to wear the stars on our clothes because we're Jewish."

"Yes," answered Tutti, trying to follow what Pappi was saying.

"And you had to change schools to be educated with other Jewish children," continued Heinz.

"Yes, Pappi."

"And we had to leave our apartment and come live here in this—" he paused, searching for the right words, "this godforsaken place."

"Yes, Pappi. I know all that."

"Well, we had to do those things because the Germans don't like Jews. They think that they are better than we are, and they're doing things to harm us."

"I know, Pappi. I've heard you and Mammi talking. *Everybody* talks about it. But what does that have to do with Popje's wobbly head?" Something was wrong and she wished Pappi would just tell her what it was.

"You know Gemmeker came to our room last night," continued Heinz.

"He said we would be leaving soon. Where are we going? Can we go back home now?" Tutti asked. She could feel the tears coming to her eyes.

"I don't know where we're going yet, but I know it won't be home to Amsterdam. And that's why I put something inside your doll."

"You put something inside Popje because we're leaving?" Tutti was struggling to understand, but it didn't make sense.

"When I was in Amsterdam, Egbert de Jong gave me some cash. Then I bought Popje and hid it inside her head. You see," Heinz said, pulling his daughter closer on the small bed they were sitting on, "her head is hollow—a perfect hiding place. The money I put in here will save our lives one day. The soldiers, the Nazis, they have stolen most of our things. They have taken our home and sent us to live in this camp. This isn't a good place—and there are camps that are worse than this one. We might have to go to one of those."

"Maybe we will see Oma Flo and Opa Louis and Muttchen and Okkie," Tutti said. She wanted to be with her grandparents again, but even more, she wanted to cheer up Pappi, who seemed so sad.

"Tutti, if we are very, very lucky, maybe we will get to see your grandparents at the next camp. But we don't know where we're going yet." Heinz's voice caught for a moment. Then he continued. "I wanted to talk with you about the money inside Popje's head. If we have some hidden money, we can use it to buy food when we are hungry or pay someone to keep us safe. It's very important that we have this money, and very important that no one knows we have it."

"It's a secret? But what if someone finds out?"

"No one will find out, not if you take care of Popje. You have the most important job. It's more important than my job selling metals. You must always keep Popje safe. Wherever you go, keep her with you. Don't lose her. Don't let anyone take her from you, *no matter what.*"

"But I had to leave Roosje in that pile of suitcases when we arrived here the first time, and I never got her back. What if they make me leave Popje in a suitcase pile somewhere?"

"If they try, just cry and scream like you used to when you were a little girl," Pappi smiled. "You can do that. Then they'll say you can keep her. Do you understand me? Do you understand how important this is?"

"Yes, Pappi. I understand."

"No one can know about Popje or the money. Remember, you can't tell anyone."

"Not even Ursula?"

126

"Not even Ursula. You can't even tell Robbie."

"Does Mammi know?"

"Yes, Mammi and you and I. We are the only ones. I know you can do this, Tutti. I'm counting on you."

Tutti felt awed by the responsibility Pappi was entrusting her with. It would be hard not to tell Robbie or Ursula, but she would keep the secret and make Pappi proud of her. "I promise," she told him solemnly. "I'll take care of her and I won't let her go and I won't tell anyone."

29

The Train

September 4, 1944

❧

"Come, *Kinder*. It's time to go," said Mammi. There wasn't much conversation as they headed out the door of their little room and walked toward the train that would take them to Theresienstadt. They each had a rucksack with their essentials, and Mammi and Pappi each had a second bag as well. Tutti hugged Popje with one arm and held Robbie's hand with the other. It was a short walk, just the length of one of the large barracks and then a little ways down the main road of the camp—whose nickname, Tutti knew, was the Boulevard of Miseries. Tutti had never really thought about that name before, but as she looked around now, it made sense to her. Under a gray sky, throngs of people were headed to the train, all with grim expressions, all staring at the ground as they tried to avoid the gray mud and find the driest patches of earth to walk on.

By the tracks, everyone had to turn over their papers for the guards to examine, and a long line had formed. Each person had to be checked off the list before getting on the train. It took a long time. When the car was considered full, the large wooden door was slammed shut. There was an ear-piercing screech as the rusty door wheels dragged against the metal track, and Tutti flinched. Then the door settled into place with a dull thud. It was latched with a metal bar that could only be opened from the outside, and someone wrote a number with a piece of chalk on the side of the car that told how many people were inside.

When it was their turn to get in, Pappi climbed up first. Mammi lifted the children one by one and handed them to their father, and then she climbed up herself. Mammi and Pappi hustled Tutti and Robbie to the back corner of the boxcar, and Tutti took in her surroundings with an increasing sense of unease. It wasn't like any train she had been in before. There were no seats. There were no windows to look out. It was one big box with some straw on the floor and a small barred window high on the wall. In the middle of the car, there was a large barrel. The place smelled like a bathroom that hadn't been cleaned in months.

As people continued to climb into the already over-crowded car, the temperature rose and the crush was over-whelming. "Mammi, how long do we have to be in here?" Tutti whimpered.

"I'm not sure," was all Mammi said, as she gathered Tutti and Robbie to her side.

Among the last to climb into the car were Pappi's friends Lotte and Max Ehrlich. When Pappi waved to them from across the car, the couple pushed their way through to join the Lichtensterns in the corner.

Mammi and Pappi sat against a wall with Robbie squeezed between them, and Tutti tried to find comfort molding herself into Pappi's side. She thought that if she breathed through her mouth and shut her eyes, the trip might be bearable. She hoped Robbie wouldn't throw up. Just the thought of that made her feel as if she might throw up, too.

A page from the transport list of September 4, 1944, Westerbork to
Theresienstadt, including Heinz, Margret, Robbie, and Tutti Lichtenstern
(#413–#416)

At first, the ride was less terrible than Tutti had expected. Max, the comedian and film star who had led the Westerbork Cabaret, sat with them and told them funny stories and jokes, and they found themselves laughing in spite of their surroundings.

"You know," Max said, "being on this train reminds me of a train trip I took about five years ago. I was with my friend and we were on our way to Berlin. The gentleman sitting across from us was making conversation, and he asked us what our plans were for that evening. My friend replied, 'We're going to the theater.' But the gentleman didn't approve. 'Oh, don't go to the theater,' he told us. 'There's a boring guest artist named Meyer who is performing tonight.' So my friend answered, 'Unfortunately, I have to go to the theater.' The gentleman asked why, and my friend answered him, 'Permit me to introduce myself. My name is Meyer.'"

Robbie couldn't help but laugh through his tears.

"Tutti," continued the comedian, "do you know what one eye said to the other eye?" He paused, but Tutti didn't answer. Mr. Ehrlich continued. "It said, 'Between you and me, something smells.'"

Tutti giggled and pulled her face out from under her father's sleeve. "Please tell us another joke, Mr. Ehrlich."

Max Ehrlich did what he did best and told another joke. For the next hour, he talked and joked and talked some more. Some of what he said Tutti didn't understand, but most of it was funny. Sometimes he just made silly faces. When eventually Max Ehrlich began to sing, many of the people sitting nearby joined in or hummed along. They all knew the songs from the Westerbork Cabaret. For a while, she was able to forget a little about where she was. Then the motion of the train started to make her drowsy, and she fell asleep leaning against Pappi.

But much of the trip from Westerbork to Theresienstadt was terrible. They were on the train for two days and two nights. The people were crowded together in the boxcar and were given nothing to eat or drink. Some people had brought food with them, but that ran out before they got to their destination.

Then there was the matter of the toilet—a large barrel in the middle of the car. Tutti had looked away as much as possible when people had had to use it, but eventually she needed to use it, too.

"Mammi, I have to go to the bathroom," she whispered.

"All right. Let's go." Holding Tutti's hand, Mammi led her to the middle of the boxcar where the barrel stood.

"Mammi!" Tutti stopped moving. "I can't use that. Everyone will see me."

"Tutti, I know you're embarrassed, but it's the only toilet we have."

Then Lotte Ehrlich handed them a blanket and said, "Here, Margret, maybe this will help."

Mammi wrapped the blanket around Tutti's shoulders and let it drape down to her knees. "There you go. This will give you some privacy."

So like everyone else in the car, Tutti sat on the barrel to relieve herself. As she sat there, she couldn't decide if she wanted to keep her head out of the blanket where it was a tiny bit less stinky or hide her face under the blanket so nobody could see her. How she wished she were back in the spotless bathroom of their apartment on De Lairessestraat, with its gleaming white tile and the faint reassuring aroma of bleach.

30

The Juggler

September 6, 1944

❧

When the transport finally arrived in Theresienstadt and the train doors opened, Tutti could hear the simultaneous drawn breath of all on board. After two days in those foul conditions, they gulped in the fresh air with relief. Then the soldiers on the platform were pulling everyone roughly from the train and pushing them into a line outside the mustard-yellow buildings.

Mammi squatted down in front of her daughter and buttoned her blue coat. It was sunny but cold. The weather was starting to feel like fall. "Tutti, you have Popje, right?"

"Yes, I'm holding her as tightly as I can." Tutti tried to sound confident. She remembered the promise she'd made to Pappi. It was her job to hold on to her doll and the secret money.

During the long wait while the prisoners were processed, Tutti played with Robbie and Popje. She tried to teach Robbie how to hold Popje like a real baby and was impressed that he could be gentle with her. But all the while, she kept a close eye on Mammi and Pappi and made sure not to get separated from them.

That's how she noticed the man who joined the group— not from the train, like all the others, but from inside the camp itself. Casually, slowly, he moved through the line, then stopped beside Pappi and began to speak to him. He was whispering, and his voice was so deep that Tutti could make out only some of the words.

"Are you sure?" asked Pappi.

"I can't . . . rumor . . ." whispered the man in his baritone.

"What happened?" he asked. All the lines on Pappi's forehead were showing and the vein in his neck turned dark blue.

". . . infirmary . . . pneumonia . . ."

"What about my mother? Have you heard anything about her?"

". . . healthy . . . working as a seamstress."

Then Mammi started to ask questions. "Do you know Flo and Louis Spier? Do you have news about them?"

"Sorry. No, I don't know them," he answered. "Excuse me, I have news for some other people."

Pappi grabbed his shoulder before he walked away. "But are you sure?" he asked. His face was white. Tutti thought he might be sick.

The man shrugged his shoulders, turned his palms up, and continued walking away.

Mammi hugged Pappi, but he pulled himself away after a moment. "Margret, I must find out about my father. I can't stand here all day not knowing. I can't imagine my mother here alone—if—" His voice trailed off.

Guards with guns over their shoulders patrolled up and down, shouting at anyone who stepped out of the line or tried to move to another place. Pappi began to follow the man who had told him about his father, but his path was suddenly blocked by a guard who—holding his rifle sideways—pushed Pappi back into the mass of people.

"Heinz, isn't that Okkie's friend Ernst Keller?" Mammi asked. "See? Way over there on the other side—through the arches."

"Yes! Margret! If Keller is here, he'll certainly know about my father. We need to talk with him."

Mammi was standing on her tiptoes and waving. Pappi was shouting, "Keller, Keller!"

"Pappi, who is Keller?" asked Tutti.

"Not now, Tutti," is all he said, as he continued to shout. There was a man waving back at Mammi, who put his hand up to his ear and shook his head.

"Pappi, why are you shouting?" asked Robbie.

"Not now, *Kinder*."

Suddenly, a German armed guard walked over, pushing Mammi and Pappi back into the crowd. They were silenced instantly.

"Tutti, I need your help," Pappi said.

"Okay, Pappi." Tutti was happy to have something to do. Anything. "What can I do?"

"Wait a minute and I'll explain." Heinz searched through his small rucksack and pulled out three pieces of paper. He scribbled a note on one, crumpled them all up, and then whispered something into Margret's ear.

Margret nodded, opened her bag, and rifled through it. She reached inside and handed him a piece of string. Heinz tied it around one of the crumpled pieces of paper.

"Tutti, here, take these balls."

"Pappi, those aren't balls. Those are just crumpled pieces of paper."

"Well, for now, they're balls. I want you to play with them. You know that trick you do when you throw the balls in the air and catch them without letting them drop on the ground?"

"You mean when I juggle like a clown in the circus?" asked Tutti.

"Yes, that's it. I want you to do that with these three balls."

"But how can that help?"

"Here's the helping part. I want you to do your juggling trick and, while you do it, walk to that corner over there. You see it? Where the big arches are?"

"Yes, Pappi."

"When you reach the corner, I want you to make a mistake."

Tutti looked at her father with a question in her eyes.

"I want you to accidentally throw this ball, the one with the string, too far, and I want it to land on the other side of that arch."

"But I don't understand—"

"See Dr. Keller over there? You met him once at Okkie's house in Amsterdam. I want you to throw that ball so he can read the note that I wrote on it. But it has to look like an accident. We aren't supposed to be talking to the people on that side. Just throw it past that archway and he'll pick it up. Don't throw it right *at* him, though. I don't want the guards to get suspicious, all right?"

"I don't know if I can do it, Pappi."

"Of course you can."

"I can't."

"It won't take long—just a minute or two. I know you can do this."

"But how can I juggle while I'm holding on to Popje?" asked Tutti.

"Oh, Tuttchen. I'll hold Popje for you. Here, give her to me." Pappi took the doll. "Now take the balls."

Tutti did as she was instructed. Then, just before one of the German guards pushed her back into the line, she tossed the ball in Dr. Keller's direction. She ran back to her parents and hid behind them.

"Keep the child with you!" the guard barked at Mammi and Pappi.

After he passed by, Tutti peered out from behind her father and Pappi rumpled her hair. "Good job, Tuttchen. Here's Popje."

"Pappi, what did you write on the paper?"

He started to answer, but Mammi interrupted. "Tutti, I have another job for you."

"Okay, Mammi, what is it?"

"I need you to keep Robbie happy."

Tutti hadn't noticed, but Robbie was sulking and near tears. Tutti looked at her mother. She seemed tired and smiled weakly. Her expression was pleading.

"Okay, Mammi," she said quietly. Tutti winked at Robbie and crossed her eyes the way Max Ehrlich had done on the train.

For the next hour, the line inched forward. Mammi and Pappi whispered to each other. Tutti tucked Popje under her arm and played all the hand games she could think of with Robbie.

At last they got to the front of the line and went through the by-now familiar registration process: somebody asked questions, Pappi answered them, and somebody else typed his answers. The man asking the questions wore a yellow star like everyone else, as did the woman next to him, who was typing all the answers onto cards. Tutti stood behind Mammi with Popje in one arm and her other arm around Robbie's shoulders. She did everything she could not to be noticed. She was quiet, she stood still, and she gripped Popje so tightly that she worried her stuffing would pop out.

When Pappi was done answering questions, the man pointed toward the area where they were to be searched. Tutti felt a jolt of fear and held Popje even tighter. What if they tried to take Popje away? What if one of the guards screamed at her to leave her doll on the pile of suitcases? Would she be able to do as Pappi had asked and pretend to have a tantrum? What if the guard shot her? With wide eyes and a pounding heart, she followed Mammi to the area where women and children were searched; Pappi, with a long glance back at them, went the other way.

Tutti hated undressing in front of the police, but everyone was doing it and, thankfully, it was quick. She took off her clothes and a woman inspected them to be sure there wasn't anything sewn inside and then gave them back. When the search was done, they were let out of the barracks to the street. It was over—and no one had even looked at her doll. Tutti breathed a sigh of relief.

They had just rejoined Pappi when they heard a familiar but unexpected sound: *Phweet, Phweet, Phweet, Phweet, Phweeeeeeee!* It was Oma Flo, Opa Louis, Muttchen, and Okkie, standing on the other side of the arches and waving.

As Tutti waved back, she noticed Mammi throwing them kisses. But Pappi didn't move. He just stood for a long time smiling at his father.

31

Theresienstadt

❧

Theresienstadt was not Westerbork. It was overcrowded and filthy. Once again, they had triple bunks and no privacy. Heinz was in one of the men's barracks, and Tutti, Robbie, and Margret were in a family barracks. As Margret settled the children into the quarters where they would be living, Tutti found herself wishing they were still in their familiar spot at Westerbork—the tiny room where she and Robbie had kicked each other at night.

Still, she knew they were lucky. She had heard one of the women in line saying that some children in the camp were there without parents—either because they were orphans or because their parents had been sent to a different camp. At least she wasn't an orphan. At least her mother and father were both with her at Theresienstadt.

Once Margret had found their barracks and their bunks and stowed what few belongings they had, they went to meet up with the rest of the family. The eight of them walked together through the camp, which was as big as a small town, with five streets running east to west and seven running north to south. Flo pointed out the town square in the middle of the camp and told Tutti that the only people allowed there were the German guards. Tutti shuddered and said, "I won't ever go there, Oma."

The walk felt normal and strange all at the same time. She remembered walking with her parents and grandparents in the Vondelpark in Amsterdam—admiring the tulips, sitting in the grass, feeding the ducks. But Theresienstadt had no flowers, no grass, no ducks—just dirt and roads that crisscrossed in front of big rectangular buildings that all looked the same.

It took a couple of weeks to get used to life in Theresienstadt—or rather, to understand just how harsh and grim conditions were.

The food was bad: just watery soup and stale or moldy bread. There wasn't enough of it, and people complained about being hungry all the time, especially the elderly, who were given smaller rations. The family barracks was crowded with two rows of triple bunks that took up nearly all the available space. Altogether, some seventy or eighty people shared the room—which meant there was no privacy and that any illness would spread quickly.

Tutti learned to her dismay that everyone over the age of nine was expected to work. Mammi and Pappi started their jobs right away—Mammi's was at the mica factory and Pappi's was in a root cellar. Tutti knew only that hers was in the hospital, and in the days before she was to report for the first time, she could think about little else. They wouldn't make her care for sick people, would they? She didn't know how. She envied Robbie, who was too young to work.

At night in their barracks, Tutti could hear people talking in German and Dutch, and in languages that she didn't recognize. Mammi told her there were people here from the Netherlands, Denmark, Austria, Germany, Hungary, and Czechoslovakia. She would sit with Robbie and Tutti on her bunk and sing a song or two or tell a story.

Then she would kiss them both good night and send them up the bunk to bed—Robbie on the middle level and Tutti on the top.

The night before she was to report to the hospital, Tutti climbed into bed with tremendous anxiety. Mammi had tried to reassure her, but she could not shake her fear about what the job might entail.

Even the game played by the children in the upper bunks couldn't distract her. It was usually one of the boys who started things. Michael Finkelstein at the far end of the room would release an explosion of gas. All the children would start giggling. Then Gerd Aschenbrand would follow Michael with a long, low vibration that lasted several seconds, or Ursula Levy would join in with her clip of several short blasts. And Tutti would laugh along with everyone else—it was impossible not to, even though she knew that Mammi disapproved.

But that night, worried about the hospital, she felt like crying instead of laughing. She held Popje and stared at the ceiling for a long time until she somehow fell asleep.

32

Messengers

❧

Tutti held Popje tightly and peered into a small room, where a woman in a red sweater sat typing at a low desk. She knew she was in the right building, but was this where she was supposed to go? She had woken early that morning, ready to find out at last what she would be doing at the hospital. There was a knot in her stomach, but at least the waiting was over.

The woman in the red sweater looked up from her typing and pointed at the bench. "*Sedni!*" she said sharply. Tutti had no idea what the word meant, but she felt like a dog that had been ordered to sit, and so she sat. A minute later, the woman left, shutting the door behind her. Tutti's nervousness turned to puzzlement. Wasn't somebody going to tell her what to do? Then there was a tentative knock at the door, and a girl Tutti hadn't seen before came in and sat on the other end of the bench. She didn't say anything. She just stared straight ahead.

The girl had short hair that was neatly brushed, but it stuck out on one side. Tutti watched as she repeatedly tucked the hair behind her ear, only to have it pop back out. The girl's front teeth were a bit too big for her mouth and protruded a little when she smiled. *Wait, did she smile?* It seemed that she did for just a second.

Tutti smiled back, and the girl picked up her hand in a small wave. Tutti waved back and added, "*Hallo.*"

"*Hallo,*" said the girl in a perfect Dutch accent.

"*Wat is je naam?*" Tutti asked.

The girl simply replied, "Gaby."

Tutti was thrilled. The girl understood her. She spoke Dutch. "*Kom je uit Nederland?*" Tutti asked.

"Yes, I'm from the Netherlands," she replied, tucking her hair behind her ear again. "Are you?"

"Yes." Tutti slid closer on the bench. "I'm Tutti. I'm from Amsterdam."

"So am I," replied Gaby. "What's your doll's name?"

"Popje."

"That's a silly name for a doll, isn't it? It isn't a real name at all."

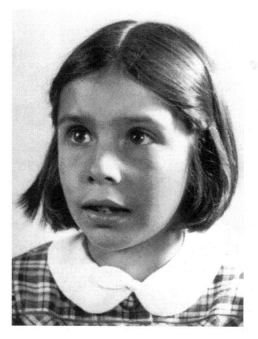

Gaby Silten

"Well, that's what I named her, and I like it," said Tutti as she hugged Popje and slid back to her original place. She had hoped that she and Gaby could be friends, but not if she was going to be mean about Popje.

Before Tutti could decide what to say or do next, the woman in the red sweater returned. "Good," she said, "you're both here. I expect you two to be on time tomorrow," she said, frowning at Gaby. "You are messengers. Now take these envelopes"—she handed one to each girl—"and bring them to the room that is indicated. Then pick up any messages the staff in that room may have and deliver those."

The job would not be hard after all! No one would expect Tutti to do more than she knew how to do. At first it was a little tricky to find her way around the building, but by the end of the day, she understood the layout perfectly. All the anxiety about the job was gone.

The next day when Tutti reported for work, Gaby was already there, waiting on the bench—and she was holding a doll of her own. It was a boy doll, wearing green woolen pants, a matching sweater, and a beret. "This is Peter," Gaby said as Tutti sat down. "He wants to be friends with Popje."

For the next few minutes, the girls played with their dolls. Then the woman in the red sweater came in with the first messages for them to deliver. As before, Tutti and Gaby were sent in different directions. But unlike that first day, and from that point on, they would often cross paths, which gave them plenty of opportunities to play. Popje and Peter became good friends—and so did Tutti and Gaby.

❧

sedni (**sehd**•nyih): sit down (Czech)

33

The Notice

Late September 1944

❧

They had been lucky so far. They had managed to stay together through Westerbork and were still all together in Theresienstadt, even though they were housed in different barracks. But the Nazis had recently been stepping up their efforts, and the transports to the East were occurring more frequently.

Just as at Westerbork, the day when the transport list was released was a time of great distress. Some people wanted to put off the potential bad news as long as possible and waited to hear the list read in the barracks. But not Heinz. He was always among the first to read the lists when they were posted. If there was bad news, he wanted to know right away.

And one evening in late September, the news was bad. Heinz felt dizzy as he read the notice. *It can't be. Nein, nein, nein!* He read the notice for a second and a third time, but there was no mistake: By the end of the week, all able-bodied men between the ages of sixteen and fifty-five were to be sent to work camps. Fifteen hundred men would be torn from their families and forced to build a new work camp in Poland. No exceptions would be made. The notice was very clear about that. *Work camps!* No one who was sent to them

This notice says that all men between the ages of 16 and 55 should prepare for transport without exception. (September 24, 1944)

was ever heard from again. They were death camps, and Heinz knew it.

He walked slowly to the barracks where his children were already sleeping and Margret was sitting on her bunk mending a shirt. "Margret—" he began, but then couldn't get the words out.

Margret could see that something was terribly wrong. "Heinz, *was ist los?* What's happening? You look awful."

"Oh, Margret—" Again, he struggled to talk, and the tears came down his cheeks.

"There's going to be another transport?" Margret really didn't need an answer—she already knew. "Who's on the list, Heinz?"

"I am."

They hugged and held each other for a long time. Both knew that these might be their last hours together. Heinz thought of so many things he wanted to say to his wife, but words were hard to find.

At dawn, Heinz looked at his sleeping children. If he was never to see them again, how could he bear it? Margret finally woke them. "Tutti, Robbie—Pappi needs to speak with you. You must wake up." They climbed down from their beds, still not fully alert, and Pappi, sobbing, enveloped them. Even before he explained that he was being sent to another camp, Tutti and Robbie were crying, too.

When it was time to report for the transport, the whole family walked with Heinz in silence. All around, the same scene was playing out: wives, mothers, sisters, and children walked with their husbands, sons, brothers, and fathers, some with stony faces, some in tears, some clinging to one another, and some praying. The Lichtensterns stayed together as long as possible, as Heinz clutched each loved one in turn.

Too soon, the soldiers herded the men into a separate area to prepare for loading. Before he got lost in the crowd, Heinz turned and offered a final wave goodbye.

❧

nein (nine): no (German)

Was ist los? (**vahs** ist lohs): What's wrong? (German)

34

Withdrawn

❧

They walked very slowly away from the train and back to the barracks area. Mammi looked sadder and more defeated than Tutti had ever seen. Her mother, who had always found a way to inspire their courage, to show them the good in any situation and help them adjust to whatever new adversity they faced, seemed overcome with sorrow. When they got back to the barracks, Mammi lay down on her bunk and put her hands over her face. Tutti didn't know what to do, but she thought it would be better not to talk to her mother right now. She took Robbie by the hand, and they went back outside to the barracks courtyard and sat there together.

How Tutti wished she could have helped Pappi. But what could she have done? His name was on the order and he had to go—the soldiers would make him. Then she looked at Popje and suddenly realized what she should have done. She should have given Popje to Pappi! He would need the money more than the rest of the family. Maybe he could have used the money to get off the train. She was so angry with herself, but it was too late. Nothing could be done about it now.

She and Robbie sat and drew pictures in the dirt and didn't say much. Tutti was waiting for Mammi to come outside—waiting to see if she would be herself again, resigned and resourceful. Pappi was gone. What if Mammi never smiled again? She suddenly realized that she should be getting to the hospital. She stood and brushed off her skirt, and that's when she heard it.

"*Phweet, Phweet, Phweet, Phweet, Phweeeeeeee!*" She looked at Robbie. Did he hear it, too? "*Phweet, Phweet, Phweet, Phweet, Phweeeeeeee!*" There it was again. They left the courtyard, walking quickly in the direction of the whistle and then breaking into a run. There was Pappi, running toward them, then kneeling down and wrapping his arms around them, pulling them close with all his strength.

Tutti and Robbie talked at the same time. "Pappi, how did you get off the train? Why did they let you come back? We have to tell Mammi!"

"Where is she? I'll explain when we find her."

And when the whole family was again reunited, this is what Pappi told them: Just before it was his turn to climb into the train, he decided to give the passport one more try. He showed it to one of the guards, and the soldier actually stopped to read it. He told Pappi to stand aside. Then, having walked away with the passport, the guard returned, handed it back with a small slip of paper, and told him to get lost.

The lifesaving slip of paper that Heinz Lichtenstern
received that day at the train

"That's actually what he said. He told me to get lost! So I grabbed my rucksack and sprinted away from the train as fast as I could," explained Pappi.

"What does the paper say?" asked Mammi.

"I don't know. I haven't even looked at it yet." Pappi pulled the little pink slip of paper out of the passport pages and read, *"Ausgeschieden* 3911 412-XXIV/7 Lichtenstern Heinz 1907-14-4."

"Ausgeschieden—withdrawn. Isn't that the most beautiful word in the world?" whispered Mammi.

❧

ausgeschieden (**ows** • geh • **shee** • dehn): withdrawn (German)

35

Washing Up

❧

"Time to wake up." Tutti could hear Mammi's voice filter through her dream, but she didn't move. It was hard to sleep here with so many people in one room. There was always somebody snoring or coughing or arguing. That's why when sleep finally came, it was hard to let go.

"Tutti, Robbie. Time to get up." Mammi was insistent.

Tutti rolled over to the edge of her bunk and looked down at her mother, who was rubbing Robbie's back. She wished her mother could tickle her back, but of course she was much too high up.

"Mammi, can't we skip it today?" she whispered.

"No, Tutti, we can't. You have to wash. Then you can go back to sleep."

It was dark in the barracks at 4 a.m., and as Tutti climbed down off the bunk bed, she accidentally stepped on Robbie's hand.

"Ow!" he screamed. "Careful, Tutti!"

Several voices all shushed Robbie at the same time. Mammi told them to be quiet, but somehow, they never made it to the washroom without someone scolding them.

Tutti turned on the faucet and studied the slow trickle of rusty water. She didn't need to touch it to know it was cold.

It was always cold. There wasn't any hot water here in Theresienstadt. That luxury was a distant memory.

She remembered how she and Robbie used to like taking a warm bath together. There would be singing and friendly splashing. Sometimes, Mammi would let them cover their faces with Pappi's foamy shaving soap and they would pretend to shave. Then, when they were done, Mammi or the nanny would wrap them in fluffy towels and pat them dry.

Now there was no warm water, no tub, no soap, and no soft towels. Tutti put her hands under the frigid trickle and splashed the water onto her face, sucking in her breath at the same time. She stuck her hand in the water again and this time used her wet finger like a toothbrush to rub the smelly film from her teeth. Finally, she splashed some water on her bottom and took the rag her mother handed her to dry off.

Robbie was trying to avoid the full regimen of washing. He complained that the water was too cold and said that he really wasn't dirty anyway.

Mammi repeated what she said every night. *"Gezicht, handen, bips, en tanden."* Face, hands, tush, and teeth: this was her minimum requirement on hygiene.

"But Mammi, why do we have to wash in the middle of the night?" Robbie whined.

"Kinder, you know how long the line is during the day. There are a hundred people sharing these three sinks. So we wash now. *Gezicht, handen, bips, en tanden.* Robbie, let me see you wash that bottom of yours."

"Mammi, it's cold." He held on to the waistband of his pants so she couldn't pull them down.

"Robbie." Her voice was getting deeper, and Tutti knew that she was losing her patience with him. "I've told you many times. It doesn't matter how cold the water is. You

The Washroom. Helga Weiss, a child survivor of Theresienstadt, drew this picture at age 12. The sign at the right means "Save water."

must wash. Washing means being clean, and being clean means staying healthy."

"I don't understand, Mammi. People don't get sick because they have dirty bottoms. People get sick when they're coughed on."

"There are lice in our clothes and there are bed bugs in the straw in our mattresses. Those bugs carry diseases, and if our bites become infected, then we will get sick. If we're sick, they might send us East. So washing is important, young man." She reached for his waistband again and yanked down his pants. "Now take that water and wash your bottom and all of those bites on your legs. If you're cold, you and Tutti can sleep on the same bed and warm each other up."

Once the children were done washing, they raced each other back to bed, covered themselves with their thin blankets, and snuggled close to sleep for a few more hours until daylight. When they awakened, Margret had already left for her job at the camp's mica factory.

36

Impossible

October 27, 1944

❧

"Heinz, isn't there anything you can do?" Margret cried.

"What can I do? I'm nobody special here." Heinz turned his empty hands up in front of him showing her his utter lack of power.

"You were able to get off the transport to Poland."

"Margret, I was able to escape the transport because of the passport. But the passport doesn't name your parents. It only has you and me and the children. I have no papers to help them. I truly wish I could, but I can't."

Heinz had had some influence in Westerbork, but here he was just one of thousands of broken Jews. There was nothing he nor anyone else could do. In the morning, Margret's parents would be getting on the train with 800 others to Poland. Rumor had it that no one returned from there. All he and Margret could hope for was that her parents would be able to stay together until the end and be comforted in knowing that the rest of the family was still, for the moment, safe.

"Shall we tell the children?" he asked.

"I don't think I can," she sputtered.

"I think we should. It isn't fair to let their grandparents just disappear," Heinz replied.

"Then you need to be the one. I can't."

"Tutti, Robbie, please come here." He gently called them.

"But we're in the middle of a game," whined Robbie.

"I know, but this is important," insisted Heinz.

"Okay, coming," said Tutti.

"Tutti, when we get back, it's my turn." Robbie was still thinking about their game. He was going on and on to his sister about how he was going to win as he climbed down off the top tier of the bunk.

"Robbie, I need you to listen to me." Heinz struggled to find the right words.

"What is it, Pappi?" asked Tutti.

"I want to tell you something." He hesitated. He wanted to tell the children that their grandparents were being sent East. He wanted to give them time to say goodbye . . . and to grieve.

"What is it, Pappi?" asked Robbie.

He wanted to be truthful with them—to give them a chance to ask questions. But how do you tell children something like this? How do you explain this horror? They'd already had a terrible time when they thought he was going East. At last he realized he couldn't tell them anything.

"Oh, never mind," Margret interrupted. "Go back to your game, children."

They scurried back up to the top bunk while Margret buried her face in Heinz's shoulder. "We can't tell them," she whispered. "This will have to wait. It will wait until they're older, much older."

Heinz stood up and told the children that he and Margret were going to visit Oma Flo and Opa Louis until curfew.

"Give them a hug for me," said Tutti.

"Me too," added Robbie.

"We will, *Kinder,*" he answered. "We'll give them the biggest hugs ever."

A page from transport list EV, dated October 28, 1944, Theresienstadt to Auschwitz, with Louis and Flora (Flo) Spier (#1133 and #1134)

37

Tutti Helps Out

❧

Tutti put on her blue woolen coat. The sleeves were too short, and she had lost one of the buttons. "Mammi, I'm going to get our dinner now." Tutti picked up the wooden carrier with its two metal pots. The contraption had a handle with a tray underneath, like a carpenter's toolbox, which allowed one person to carry several portions at once.

"Don't forget the ration cards," Mammi said. She was lying on her bunk with an arm across her face. "They won't give you anything without them."

Tutti took the worn brown cards with each family member's name and tucked them into her pocket. "I'll be back soon," she said.

She was glad to be helping Mammi, but she was also glad to have a reason to get out of the barracks. It had been two weeks since Oma Flo and Opa Louis had been sent to Poland on one of the transports, and her mother had been suffering. She would be herself for hours at a time, but then she'd withdraw and lie on the bed in silence. Pappi said that Mammi might be sad for a long time, and that they must all try to be as helpful as possible.

Tutti sang her old jump rope songs and hopped on one foot as she walked to the food distribution area. When she got to the line, she saw Gaby arriving with her own family's carrier.

The line was always long. People pushed to get their measly rations, and it was better to stand with a friend. Gaby and Tutti liked waiting together. They put their food trays on the ground between their feet and played a hand game, clapping their hands rhythmically as they chanted rhymes.

"Girls, move up," snarled an old man. The old people were impatient. Their rations were smaller than those of the younger people. Pappi had explained that anyone who could work got a bit more food. She wondered now whether Flo and Louis were getting enough food in the camp in Poland, but she knew she wouldn't ask Mammi about it.

When they got to the front of the line, Tutti and Gaby presented their ration cards. One woman took the cards, stamped them, and handed them back, while another woman plopped a ladleful of soup into each pot. Usually, the thin broth had a few scraps of vegetables. Tonight, it had only a few potato peels. The girls put their bread allotments into their pockets and quickly moved away to avoid being pushed.

They said goodbye at Gaby's barracks and Tutti continued on her way, hopping and chanting once again. "Go in the spinning loop, out you go from the loop," she sang, thinking of the games she had played in Amsterdam. Somehow she didn't notice the stone in her path, and she stumbled against it. She didn't fall, but to her horror, the precious soup sloshed over the edges of the pots and dripped through the tray onto the ground.

Tutti hurried back to the barracks and placed the tray on the small stool by the foot of Mammi's bed. She felt angry with herself. Instead of helping, she had lost some of their dinner. She hoped her mother wouldn't notice, but she could see Mammi's eyes move from the pots, to the tray, to

Standing in the Queue in Front of the Kitchen. Helga Weiss, a child survivor of Theresienstadt, drew this picture at age 12 of prisoners waiting in line to pick up their rations.

the wet splotch on Tutti's coat.

Mammi pursed her lips and shook her head. "Not again, Tuttchen."

"Sorry, Mammi!" Tears sprang to her eyes.

"You have to walk carefully. This is all we get for the four of us." Then her voice grew gentler, more like what Tutti thought of as her real voice. "I know it was an accident. Come, let's eat." When Mammi got up from her bunk, Tutti hugged her, hoping she realized how sorry she was.

Before the family sat down to dinner, Mammi took a small loaf of stale bread and used it to soak up the broth still in the tray. Every drop was precious.

Tutti watched her mother ladle the usual portions for Robbie and her, but Mammi and Pappi went with less. *Like Oma Flo and Opa Louis,* she thought. She promised herself she would be more careful from now on.

38

Contraband

❧

Tutti found herself thinking about food all the time. When she and Gaby played with their dolls, they gave them fancy dinners with their favorite treats.

"Let's pretend they're having a feast because the queen is visiting," Tutti said one afternoon as they played on the steps of the hospital, waiting for their next assignments. "Popje can be the queen and Peter can be the cook."

"No, Peter is Prince Henry. And his favorite thing to eat is roasted chicken and rolls with butter."

"And the rolls will be warm so the butter will melt on them," Tutti said. "And they'll also have fried potatoes, with little bits of onion."

"And they'll have gingerbread with white icing for dessert."

"And not just gingerbread for dessert, but some little cakes, too!" Tutti was remembering her outing with Uncle Bobby so long ago. "All different colors with little silver balls on them and jam inside."

"And pancakes with strawberries and whipped cream."

"And lemonade."

"Yes, lemonade. That will be perfect for the queen and the prince," Gaby agreed.

✣   ✣   ✣

Food was also on the mind of Heinz, who worked in the root cellar sorting vegetables. Every day, he pulled rotten potatoes out of the bins and put them in a pile; these would later be brought to the kitchen to be made into soup for the prisoners. The fresh vegetables were saved for the Germans. As he sorted the carrots, turnips, radishes, and beets, a guard watched to make sure he didn't eat or steal anything.

One day, he arrived at the root cellar to find a new guard. That wasn't unusual, but the fact that this man was so familiar to Heinz threw him into a tailspin. *Where have I seen him before?* he wondered. Just as he was searching his memory, the guard faced Heinz, tipped his hat, and said, *"Guten Morgen,* Herr Lichtenstern." His mannerisms, his voice —it all came rushing back to him.

Years ago, before the war, Heinz had frequented the Hotel Bristol whenever he was in Berlin for work. It was one of the most prestigious in the city and attracted guests from around the world. He was always generous with the staff, especially when the service was superb, which was precisely what the Bristol was known for.

This guard in the root cellar of Theresienstadt had been the hotel's headwaiter!

Heinz gathered his emotions and returned to the present moment.

"Guten Tag, Herr Schmidt," he replied.

"Table for one?" asked the guard.

Heinz couldn't believe it. This man was actually joking with him. *Should I joke back? Would he be offended if I didn't?* Finally, he answered, "Yes, table for one."

Over the course of the next few days, Heinz and Schmidt talked quite a lot, and Heinz let him know that he was not alone at Theresienstadt—that his wife, young children, and parents were prisoners, too. And then a wonderful thing happened.

"Lichtenstern, it's time for my break. I forgot my cigarettes, and I'm going to get them. I'll be gone for twenty minutes."

"Yes, sir," said Heinz. He looked at the guard uncertainly.

"Your children are hungry, yes?" And with that, the guard left him alone surrounded by sacks of food.

Heinz understood. Schmidt, whom he had tipped so well, was now repaying the favor. Heinz grabbed a handful of beets and shoved them in his pocket, but his pockets were small and didn't hold much. *To hell with pockets*, he thought. *I'll put the vegetables down my pant legs.* He had taken to wearing his woolen ski pants in the winter, and they were baggy with tight cuffs at the ankles. He put as many carrots and turnips in his pants as he could without it being noticeable, and he walked quickly to the family barracks. Margret would have returned from her early shift, and he was eager to share the bounty with her right away.

When Heinz got back to the cellar, he saw to his relief that the guard was still on his break. He sat down on a barrel of rotten potatoes, amazed at what had just transpired. A few minutes later, Schmidt appeared with a smile and ordered Heinz to get to work.

This scene repeated itself many times that winter. But one day, as Heinz was hurrying to deliver his contraband, he came around a corner and literally bumped into two German soldiers.

"Idiot!" shouted one soldier.

Margret and Heinz wearing baggy ski pants before the war (1937)

"Where are you going in such a hurry?" shouted the other.

"To the barracks, sir." Heinz replied, averting his eyes and trying to quell his panic. What if the soldiers questioned him about the bulges in his pant legs? Would they beat him? Would they shoot him right here for stealing vegetables?

"Show us your papers," said the first soldier.

Heinz reached into his shirt pocket and pulled out his camp identification card. The soldier studied it for quite some time.

"Heinz Lichtenstern. This says that you were a businessman. What was your business?"

"Metals." He could hardly get the word out. He didn't know what these two guards might do.

"I have metal bullets in my gun, Hans," the soldier said to his partner. "Shall I give this metals dealer some metal in his head?" And he lifted his gun and pointed it at Heinz's face.

Heinz was paralyzed. Were they going to shoot him for not looking where he was going? What if they found the vegetables? His stomach churned and he thought he might vomit, but instead, he felt a warm trickle down his leg. He had soiled himself—lost control of his bowels in his terror.

"What's that stench?" Hans asked his partner.

"It's Jew. This is a stinking Jew," said the other soldier. "Get out of here, stinking Jew. You're fouling our air." Hans pushed Heinz to the ground, and his partner hit him with the butt of his gun. He seemed to forget his idea of using a bullet. His intent was humiliation, and he had succeeded.

When Heinz arrived at the barracks, Margret saw that he was as white as a sheet except for the purple goose egg that appeared on his head.

"Heinz, what happened? Are you all right?" She rushed to him to examine his forehead.

"I wasn't watching where I was going. I actually walked right into a guard. I was so frightened, I—I soiled myself. I've ruined the vegetables."

"Heinz, I'm sorry!" She lifted his hair to get a better look at the bump. "It's not bleeding, thankfully. I wish we had some ice to put on it, but it will go down eventually. And don't worry about the vegetables," she said, still in the same consoling tone. "This is nothing that a good scrubbing won't take care of. Here's a rag you can use to clean yourself up. You need to get back before they miss you at the root cellar."

That night, after the vegetables were scrubbed clean and simmered in water on the wood stove in the barracks, the family had vegetable soup for dinner. Heinz and Margret knew that the children needed the vitamins and the calories. They didn't tell them what their father had gone through to provide them with this meal, or what their mother had gone through to prepare it.

✸

guten Morgen (**goo**•tuhn **mohr**•guhn): good morning (German)

guten Tag (**goo**•tuhn **tahk**): good day (German)

39

Scavengers

❧

Robbie, too, was often hungry, and as a result had become a skilled scavenger. He seemed to possess some sixth sense that allowed him to find all sorts of edible treasures that Tutti never noticed.

When Robbie told Tutti one day that he'd found a treat, she grabbed Popje and followed her brother. She didn't know where he was taking her, but she trusted him. When they came to the area where the soldiers spent their breaks, however, Tutti hesitated.

"Robbie, I don't think we should be here."

"But this is where the treat is."

"I know, but there are so many soldiers."

"Don't be a scaredy-cat. It'll be okay, I promise."

The soldiers laughed and talked in loud voices. Some smoked cigarettes and several were eating. Tutti saw one with a chocolate bar, and a few had oranges.

"So where is the treat, Robbie?" Tutti asked.

"You'll see."

A moment later, one of the soldiers threw his orange peel into the street. Robbie ran over, grabbed the peel, and handed it to his sister. In the next five minutes, Robbie scooped up peels from three more oranges.

The children didn't linger. They ran down the street to savor their orange peels in private, away from the soldiers. Tutti couldn't believe how delicious they were. Why would anyone throw them away? Back in Amsterdam, of course, she had always thrown away the peels without thinking. Now she squeezed them to spray the fresh, citrusy scent into her face, and ate every bit of every piece of skin, the orange and the white. The peels were tough and satisfying, bitter and sweet at the same time.

❧ ❧ ❧

As for Margret, she thought about food all the time—not simply because she was hungry, but because she had children, a husband, and in-laws to take care of. As for her own parents, she dared not think about them too often; if they were alive, they were certainly starving, but there was nothing she could do for them. It was her family here at Theresienstadt that she needed to feed.

For a while, the vegetables that Heinz stole had made a difference. It was good to be able to nourish her family; even scrubbing the filthy vegetables after Heinz's accident had felt purposeful and right. She was a mother, and providing food for her children was her job. But after that day, Heinz was afraid to go on stealing, and eventually a new guard was stationed in the root cellar and the opportunity was lost. So they were back to the camp's soup, weak and watery and insubstantial.

Sometimes she admired Robbie's ingenuity in tracking down and pocketing edible scraps for the family. But she also wanted her son to learn right from wrong—and to stay safe. How was that possible, though, in a place like Theresienstadt, where hunger and danger were always with them? And so went the constant tug of war in Margret's mind. "This camp is not a place for children," she would often say to Heinz. It was shorthand for all the emotions she couldn't put into words.

One day, as she was carrying some bread that she had put aside for Heinz's parents, Robbie asked, "Mammi, why do we always bring our bread to Okkie and Muttchen? Don't they have their own?"

"They do, but when you visit someone, it's nice to offer a gift," replied Margret. "When you're all grown up and you go to someone's house for a visit, I want you to bring a few flowers or a little something to eat. It's the polite thing to do."

"But I'm *hungry*," complained Robbie. "Can't we bring them something else?"

"What else would you suggest, Robbie? We don't have any flowers here. Besides, when we give them the bread, they'll be so happy. And then, you know what they always do with it, don't you?" asked Margret.

"I know," answered Tutti. "Muttchen will take the bread and say, 'Thank you, but that wasn't necessary. It's better to give it to the children.'" Tutti was good at imitating her grandmother's melodic voice. "Then she'll tear off two pieces for Robbie and me and save just a little for herself and Okkie."

"That's what I mean," said Robbie. "Why should we give them the bread if they're just going to give it back?"

They had almost reached the barracks where Heinz's parents lived when Margret stopped short. "Because we're civilized," she said in a low, intense voice. "No matter where we live or how little we have, we must treat others with respect and kindness. We share with others. We say *please* and *thank you*."

Just then, as they came around a corner, they were startled to see a train on the tracks. It was unexpected, as trains didn't usually stop in the camp at this time of day. But many unexpected things had been happening lately. Instead of sending Jews East, now the Germans were bringing them *to* Theresienstadt *from* the East. The Germans were evacuating the camps in Poland and Germany ahead of the advancing Russian army. They were afraid the Allies would find out what had really been happening in those camps. Margret had seen those Jews from the East coming off the trains before—emaciated and sick, close to death from starvation or typhoid—and it was evidence that places far worse than Theresienstadt existed.

"Mammi, I hear people crying on the train," Robbie said.

"Why are they still on the train?" asked Tutti.

"I'm not sure, *Kinder*."

Tutti thought of their own train trip, and of the transports that came and went each week. "Maybe they're hungry, Mammi."

Without thinking, Margret took the measly loaf of bread she was holding and threw it into the small window of one of the cattle cars.

Instantly, there was a cry of voices. Someone yelled, "Bread!" And then another person yelled, "Mine." And somebody screamed as if he were in pain. They were battling over the stale bread. The people in the cattle car had been reduced to fighting like animals, and the three Lichtensterns couldn't bear their anguish.

Robbie pulled his mother by the hand. "Let's go. I don't want to stay here." Then he said solemnly, "Now we have no bread to share with Muttchen and Okkie."

40

Liberation

May 8–9, 1945

❧

For days, the Jews on the upper floors of the camp buildings had watched cars and trucks speeding by. The Nazis were trying to escape before the Russians arrived. Then one evening, news of Germany's unconditional surrender reached Theresienstadt. The war was over. Germany had lost.

But within hours, Theresienstadt itself turned into a war zone. As the German army retreated, they threw hand grenades into the camp and shot at anyone who tried to flee. Then the Russian army accidentally shelled a building inside the camp. The war may have been over, but not for the Jews of Theresienstadt.

When the sound of gunfire seemed uncomfortably close, Heinz decided they had to act. "Margret, take the children to the cellar!" he said. "We need to get out of here!"

Margret didn't argue. She grabbed Tutti's hand, put her other arm around Robbie's waist, and guided them to the basement of the barracks. Heinz ran upstairs to find his parents. His father was weak with hunger and his mother was trying to get him out of bed. Together, Jenny and Heinz picked Okkie up and coaxed him down the stairs to the basement. They joined Margret and the children in the small underground room.

The walls were gray cement, with one small street-level window along the top. About thirty people sat in silence on the benches that ringed the room and listened to the chaos outside. Every once in a while, Heinz would stand on the bench to peer out the window. He couldn't see much, mostly just wheels from vehicles driving on the street and feet of people running by. It was what he heard that worried him the most—gunshots and small explosions. He didn't know if the Germans were shooting Jews or if the Russians were killing Germans. Either way, he didn't want to be in the middle of it.

The cellar was claustrophobic, but the fighting outside gave no indication of letting up, and nobody left. Robbie was restless and kept asking questions.

"Mammi, can't we go outside now?"

"Robbie, it isn't safe," Margret answered.

"Can't we at least go upstairs to a room with windows so we can watch?"

"No, Robbie! We cannot go anywhere until everyone out there stops shooting!" Heinz was firm in his answer.

✤　✤　✤

They emerged from their hiding place the following evening. The Russian army had driven its trucks and tanks through the middle of the camp. There was no sign of German soldiers. People lined the streets—waving handkerchiefs, shouting with joy, and crying with relief.

Heinz wasn't quite as overjoyed as those around him. He knew the reputation of the Russians: savages. He wished the Americans or the Canadians had been the ones to liberate Theresienstadt. Margret, Heinz, and his parents hung back on the sidewalk behind the throngs of people, holding the children close. They feared this army almost as much as the Nazis.

"Mammi, I can't see," Robbie complained. He tugged his mother's hand, trying to get to the edge of the sidewalk for a better view of the parade of tanks.

"Stop," replied Margret.

"I want to see them!" he insisted, as he yanked his hand free and pushed his way through the crowded sidewalk to the curb.

"Robbie!" shrieked Margret.

Heinz let go of Tutti and tried to follow his son, but it was impossible. The seven-year-old scooted under elbows and between legs. "Robbie, come back here!" he shouted. He could just make out the top of his son's head. The small boy stood at the curb watching the tanks roll by.

Robbie ignored his parents' frantic calls, or maybe he couldn't hear them. On tiptoe and craning their necks, Heinz and Margret spotted him standing tall and saluting the passing tanks, his small hand angled against his forehead. They saw, too, when a soldier in one of the trucks hopped down, handed him a chocolate bar, and lifted him into the truck.

Margret screamed, "Please! Please don't take my boy!"

Heinz yelled, "Robbie, Robbie!"

But the truck disappeared around the corner.

Heinz pushed his way through the crowd, following the trucks, but he was too late. It was impossible to tell which truck he was in and where it had gone.

Margret was sitting on the curb, sobbing on Okkie's shoulder, when he returned. How could he console her? He knew what she was thinking. Could they have survived the war and the camps and the Nazis, only to lose their son to the liberating army?

It was Tutti who saw that her brother had not in fact been taken away. "Mammi! Pappi! He's over there!" Tutti

172

Prisoners welcome Russian soldiers at Theresienstadt (May 1945)

was pointing down the road, where a grinning Robbie was slowly working his way back to them.

They all looked up in disbelief. Margret wiped her eyes. Tutti was right. Robbie was coming toward them. Heinz pushed his way through the masses of people to get to his son. When he reached him, he grabbed him in a bear hug. "Don't ever do that to us again!" he cried.

"I'm sorry, Pappi, but did you see? The soldiers took me for a ride on their truck."

"Yes, I saw. You have to promise me that you won't run away from me again. It was very dangerous."

"They were nice. Look what they gave me," he said, holding out a box.

Heinz hadn't noticed the box before. "Let's give that to Mammi."

When they opened it, they saw that it was full of oranges, chocolate, sardines, and a large loaf of dark Russian bread. They laughed and cried as they passed the food around in celebration.

41

The Long Road

June 1945

❧

What Tutti couldn't understand was why, if the war was over, they couldn't go home. It had been a month since the Russians had liberated the camp, and the family was still in Theresienstadt.

Margret tried to explain it as best she could. "One problem is that many people have typhus. If they leave, then the disease will spread all over Europe. These people have to stay here until they recover."

"But Mammi, *we* aren't sick," said Tutti.

"I know. We're here because of another problem," said Mammi. This one was more complicated to explain. The Lichtensterns were stateless. Because the Germans had revoked their citizenship, they didn't have the right to live in Germany anymore—not that she ever wanted to live in Germany again after what the Germans had done. But they hadn't become Dutch citizens, and the Dutch didn't want a flood of refugees.

"Then why don't we just go somewhere else? There has to be somewhere better than here, Mammi," said Tutti.

"You're right. But there are other problems, too," Mammi sighed. "The roads and the railroad lines have been damaged or destroyed by bombs in the war. So it's very hard to travel. And remember, we're not the only ones who want to go home."

❧ ❧ ❧

At long last, the day came when Mammi told them, "We're leaving today and finally going back to Amsterdam!"

"I can't wait to sleep in my own bed tonight! I won't have to share with Robbie, will I?" asked Tutti.

"And I won't have to share with Tutti, right?" chimed in Robbie.

"*Kinder*, we are just starting the trip. We certainly won't make it all the way home to Amsterdam in one day. We'll see where we sleep tonight when tonight comes," Mammi told the children. "You need to be patient."

How patient they would need to be not even Margret could have anticipated. From the beginning, it seemed as if anything that could delay their journey did. First, it was bad weather. Thunderstorms meant that they had to spend the first night only about a hundred miles from Theresienstadt at an old hospital. Second, there were simply not enough trucks to carry all the people who needed to travel. And when trucks did become available, the damaged roads slowed them down. But with every passing day, they were getting closer.

❧ ❧ ❧

Once again, they had been on the road almost a full day. Robbie, who was very sleepy, managed to wiggle his way onto the floor and doze alongside the other passengers' feet. Tutti wanted to look outside, but the truck was all closed up and the air was hot and sticky. Eventually, she fell asleep, lying across her parents' and grandparents' laps and hugging Popje.

When Mammi woke her, it was dark.

"Are we home yet?" she asked.

"No, Tuttchen. We are in Dobřany. Let's go inside. There are nice beds here with clean sheets."

As they walked inside, Tutti noticed that they were in a fine building with a long hallway and several rooms. Tutti shared a bed with Muttchen, while Robbie and Mammi climbed into another bed. The sheets were white and the pillows were soft and there weren't any scratchy bedbugs. It was so comfortable, she didn't care that she had to share.

In the morning, Tutti saw that Pappi and Okkie were sleeping on the floor, both snoring quietly. They seemed to have made themselves mattresses out of blankets. There must not have been enough beds. While that couldn't have been too comfortable, Tutti imagined that given the peaceful look on Pappi's face, he was having a sweet dream.

42

New Friends

June 11, 1945

❧

After five days in Dobřany, the family was on the move again. This time they went by American trucks to an airfield outside Pilsen, where they had been told they could fly out of Czechoslovakia.

"Mammi, I'm all wet. Why do we have to be outside in the rain?" complained Robbie.

"I'm soaked too," added Tutti.

"I know, *Kinder*," replied Mammi as she pulled the children to her side, protecting them from the downpour. "We want to get closer to home, and the Americans thought that we could fly from here to the Netherlands. But the planes are grounded."

"Why?" asked Robbie.

"Because the pilot can't see well in a storm."

All they could do was wait. Tutti was shivering and hungry. After spending the day on the open field in the rain, they were given a place to sleep on the cold, hard floor of a building that had been converted into barracks. There were no beds or blankets and there wasn't much to eat.

The next morning, the Allied Expeditionary Forces provided a breakfast of dry bread. The children were cranky, and the adults were crankier. Tutti was bored beyond belief.

"Mammi, it stopped raining. Can we go outside?"

Margret looked out the window and smiled. "Robbie, Tutti. Come with me." She signaled Heinz, Okkie, and Muttchen to follow. "*Kinder*, I have a job for you. Do you see those two American soldiers standing over there?"

"Yes, Mammi," they said together.

"When they're done with their cigarettes, they'll drop the butts on the ground. I want you two to pick them up. If we collect enough butts, your father and grandparents can have their own cigarettes tonight."

The two soldiers wore crisp, clean uniforms. One was tall and the other was short. Tutti decided the tall soldier was quite handsome. His square jaw was topped with a friendly smile. Dimples defined his cheeks and his wide forehead led to dark hair that was combed back in a wave.

As Tutti was admiring the handsome soldier, the short one dropped his cigarette butt on the ground. Robbie scooped it up, just as he had done in the camp with the orange peels, and raced back to his mother. The shocked soldier didn't know what to make of the speedy child. The tall soldier, also finished with his smoke, dropped it on the ground and then watched as Tutti whisked it up. They stared as Margret opened the nubs and emptied the remaining tobacco into a handkerchief.

"Excuse me," said the handsome soldier. "Would you like a cigarette?" He held out his pack toward Margret and Heinz.

Margret's face turned red. She couldn't answer. Tutti looked at her proud and embarrassed mother and wondered what she was thinking at that moment.

Heinz was the first to speak. "Thank you. Thank you very much. It's been so long since we've been able to smoke."

"You speak English very well. You don't have to pick up trash. Come with us. We can get you a whole pack," said the shorter soldier.

Heinz held out his hand. "I am Heinz Lichtenstern, and this is my wife, Margret, and my parents, Oscar and Jenny."

"And who are these two nimble children?" asked the tall one.

"This is Tutti and her brother, Robbie," answered Margret. She had finally found her voice. When Tutti heard her name, she stood tall and smiled at the good-looking American.

"Where are my manners?" said the tall soldier. "Let me introduce myself. I am Sergeant Lloyd Miller and this is my friend, Corporal Stanley Greenberg."

"Where are you from?" asked Corporal Greenberg.

"That's a long story," replied Heinz. "We've been in Theresienstadt for the past nine months. And before that, at a camp in the Netherlands."

"You're refugees from the Netherlands? I'm Jewish, too. What you must have been through," he said, shaking his head. "Please, come with us. Let's feed these children, and then we'll find those cigarettes we promised."

That was the beginning of a wonderful friendship. Sergeant Miller and Corporal Greenberg brought the Lichtensterns back to their own quarters and treated them to extra rations. They explained that they'd only recently left the United States, as they were replacements in the 8th Armored Division. They hadn't actually met any survivors yet, so they were full of questions about the past five years and life in the camps. They wanted to know about the conditions and how the family had survived. In turn, the Lichtensterns were full of questions that the soldiers could answer—and one

Sgt. Lloyd Miller posing in front of a captured German plane (June 1945)

that they couldn't: How much of Europe was destroyed? Was Amsterdam intact? What happened to Margret's parents who were sent East?

Margret translated some of what the soldiers said for the children, but mostly Tutti just enjoyed the extra food and the adventure of being able to spend time with their new friends.

They sat with the G.I.s on their bunks and talked past midnight. Robbie fell asleep under Miller's bunk, and Tutti dozed off holding Popje and dreaming about Lloyd Miller.

❖   ❖   ❖

The next morning, the soldiers presented the family with a hearty breakfast of real bean coffee and bread piled high with thick swipes of butter and cold cuts. They also gave them a supply of sugar, cocoa, soap, cigarettes, and, to the delight of the children, chewing gum.

Tutti and Robbie had never had chewing gum before. Robbie unwrapped a piece and promptly popped it in his mouth. *"Dank u. Mag ik er nog een?"*

"Nee, dat mag je niet," answered Mammi.

Corporal Greenberg turned to her for a translation.

"I'm afraid he is asking for another piece, but I told him no. I'm sorry." Tutti could tell that her mother was embarrassed again.

"Already, little man? You didn't swallow it, did you?" asked Corporal Greenberg, with Margret as his translator.

"Yes, it was delicious," answered Robbie.

"Haven't you had gum before? You aren't supposed to swallow it. It's just for chewing. Just keep chewing until the flavor is all gone. Then you can throw it out," explained the corporal.

"What do I do with it when it's time to go to sleep?" asked Tutti.

181

"American children put their gum behind their ear to save it for the next day," joked Corporal Greenberg.

The rest of that afternoon was spent with the American soldiers. They took several pictures of the Lichtensterns, and Lloyd Miller gave the adoring Tutti a couple of snapshots of himself.

The next morning when Tutti woke up, her hair was all tangled. "Mammi, I can't find my gum," complained Tutti.

"It's in your hair, Tuttchen. How on earth did it get there?" asked Mammi.

"Corporal Greenberg told me to sleep with it behind my ear." Tutti started to cry.

"Oh, Tuttchen—he was only joking! You were supposed to throw it out, not save it." Mammi pulled her close and hugged her. "I guess it's time you had a haircut anyway. Let's see if someone around here has any scissors."

After nine months in Theresienstadt, and after numerous hardships on the road back to Amsterdam, the kindness and generosity of these two Americans was something no one in the family ever forgot.

43

A Doctor's Care

❧

On the afternoon of their fifteenth day of travel, the family arrived at a refugee camp in Maastricht. They were in the Netherlands at last. But this place was a disappointment. Mammi actually made them throw out their soup that evening because it was inedible and would have made them sick.

The next stop on their journey was a refugee camp in Sittard, 120 miles from home. Pappi explained to Tutti and Robbie that they would be repatriated here. What that meant was another lengthy registration process. First they had to stand in a long line, and then Pappi had to answer questions and wait while someone typed his answers.

Would they ever be able to go anywhere without lining up like this? Tutti wondered. Here, it was American soldiers who asked the questions, typed the answers, and handed each person a card containing their vital information: name, birthdate, address before the war, nationality, and languages spoken. Then they all lined up again for a medical examination. When finally it was Tutti's turn, the doctor listened to her heart and lungs; checked her eyes, ears, nose, and throat; examined her skin; made some notations on a card; and then declared, "You have lice. You'll need to report to the delousing area." He didn't even glance at her when he said this.

Tutti's AEF DP (Displaced Person) registration card

"Mammi, do I have to go alone?" she asked.

Hearing the anxiety in Tutti's voice, the doctor finally made eye contact with her. "Oh, sweetheart, you don't have to go alone. Wait right here for the rest of your family. You can all go together." Then he turned to Mammi. "Forgive me, ma'am. I didn't mean to frighten your daughter. It's been a grueling day. And there are *so* few children. I forgot my bedside manners."

✤   ✤   ✤

To treat Tutti's and Robbie's head lice, a thick, syrupy balm that looked like molasses was spread on their scalps. Unfortunately, it smelled like gasoline.

After that ordeal, the family was issued medical clearances and registration cards and then settled into the cloisters of a convent. While the Allied Expeditionary Forces were surely doing their best, conditions for the multitudes of refugees were dreadful.

When Tutti went to sleep that night, she was upset about the clogged toilets, deplorable food, and smelly hair treatment. But, she realized, that nice doctor *had* said he was sorry.

Thinking back to every new rule they'd had to endure under the Nazis and every move they'd made, Tutti recalled how often Mammi would remind her that change was hard. But this one felt good.

Maybe all changes weren't so bad, after all.

44

Welcome Home

June 30, 1945

❧

Heinz was desperate to get his family home.

After having been in Sittard for several days, he told an American sergeant, "Before this damn war began, I had been living in Amsterdam for four years." He had wanted to talk with the captain in charge but had been advised he was unavailable. "I had a nice home. My son was born there, for God's sake. He's a Dutch citizen and he deserves to go home."

"Maybe we can make arrangements for your son."

"He's only seven years old!"

"Please sit down," said the sergeant. "Let's see what we can do."

Heinz relaxed a little at those words and handed the sergeant his papers: his AEF displaced persons registration card, Dutch ID card with the big J on it, Jewish Council card, DP index card—and even his Westerbork work card. The sergeant looked over the documents.

"I'm sorry, Mr. Lichtenstern, but I need more if I'm to convince the Dutch authorities."

Heinz, who felt himself losing his temper again, bit his tongue, let out a long sigh, and quietly said, "We've been through so much . . ."

"Why don't you tell me how you made it this far? Maybe there's something I can use," offered the sergeant.

So Heinz told him their story. Tears came to his eyes as he recalled the night when he found himself on the Auschwitz transport list and his miraculous release at the last minute because of the Paraguayan passport.

"What? Wait a minute!" interrupted the American. "You have a Paraguayan passport?"

"Well, yes, but we're not really Paraguayan."

"That doesn't matter! If you have a passport, then you are not stateless. Where is it?"

"Here—I have it right here!" Heinz reached into his bag and produced the small booklet.

The American laid it on the table in front of him and opened it. He smiled as he unfolded the large page with the four pictures. "You're in luck!" he shouted, energetically crossing out the line on Heinz's registration card that indicated "stateless" and inserting "Paraguay" in large block letters. "This is all we need," he said. "Tell your wife to pack. We're sending you home!"

"What about my parents? May they come with us?" asked Heinz.

"Do they have a Paraguayan passport, too?" asked the American.

"No, but I can vouch for them."

The American looked at Heinz with a weak smile and shook his head. "I'm afraid they'll have to wait here until all of this business about people being stateless is sorted out."

Within twenty-four hours, the Lichtensterns were boarding a train to Amsterdam.

"We'll find a way to get you home, too," said Heinz, as he hugged his mother and father goodbye. This was their fifth tearful farewell since the Netherlands had been invaded.

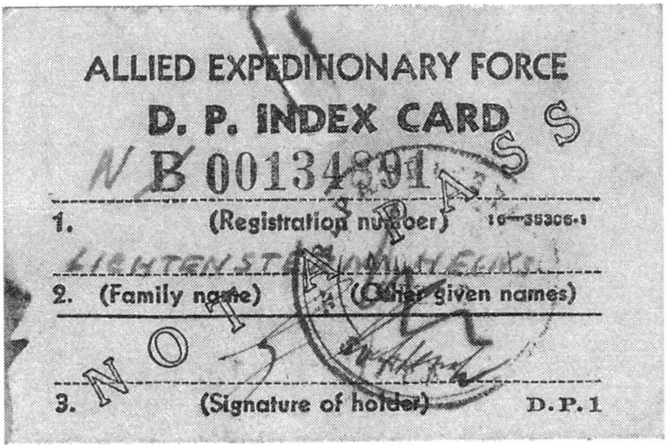

ALLIED EXPEDITIONARY FORCE

D. P. INDEX CARD

B 00134891

1. (Registration number) 16—35306-1

2. (Family name) (Other given names)

3. (Signature of holder) D.P.1

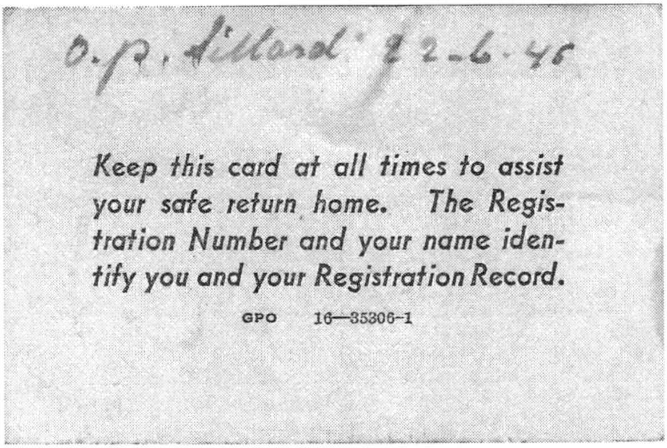

Keep this card at all times to assist your safe return home. The Registration Number and your name identify you and your Registration Record.

GPO 16—35306-1

Heinz's AEF DP (Displaced Person) index card

❧   ❧   ❧

On the train to Centraal Station, the family looked out the window, lost in thought. They were exhausted from days of traveling and mostly wretched accommodations, all filled with emotions that were hard to put into words.

And then they saw it: Amsterdam! There was the Victoria Hotel with its white façade and wrought-iron balconies. Beyond was Dam Square with the Royal Palace and the beautiful canals that ringed the city.

"Tutti, Robbie, we're home!" cried Margret. There was relief and excitement in her voice. "Heinz, try to make some calls," she said, as they stepped outside into the sunshine, "and find a place for us to stay. We'll be waiting for you on this bench."

So Heinz went back inside the station and found a clerk at the ticket desk who was willing to let him use a telephone. But the calls proved fruitless. He either got no answer or a stranger picked up. His friends had moved—or worse.

By now, he had heard the news that the Nazis had murdered millions of Jews. He wondered how many of his friends were among them. He had hoped never to leave Amsterdam, and he had done everything in his power to get his family back here. But it wasn't the same city as the one they'd left. He wondered if it could ever be the same again.

When Heinz could reach neither friends nor work colleagues, he at last tried his old neighbor, Adriaan Vos. Vos had been so accommodating and had volunteered to protect their valuables when they were forced to leave De Lairessestraat. They wouldn't impose on Vos for long, he told himself, just until they could find something more permanent. Surely he would be understanding and welcome them.

But that night, they ended up sleeping at the railroad station. It wasn't comfortable, but it also wasn't the worst place they had slept.

"It's still hard to believe you couldn't find anybody at all," Margret said, as she fashioned an improvised bed for the children on a baggage cart.

"The only one who answered was Adriaan Vos."

"So? Couldn't we stay with him?"

"He said he was busy preparing for dinner guests." Then Heinz lowered his voice so the children wouldn't hear. "He said he never expected to see us again."

45

Oh, Brother!

❧

By the next morning, Heinz had thrown off the gloom of the night before. He and Margret and the children were alive, the war was over, and they were back in Amsterdam. "Why don't you find the children something to eat and I'll try to make some more phone calls," Heinz said. "Yesterday, I only called people in Amsterdam. I didn't try Egbert de Jong. He's probably still in The Hague."

Unfortunately, because he couldn't find a clerk who would let him use the phone, he was forced to join the long line at the station pay phone. Heinz tried to start a conversation with some of the other men waiting to make calls, but when they noticed his German accent, they cut the conversation short. So Heinz stood in line silently and worried about what he would do if he couldn't reach Egbert.

He was deep in thought when he heard something familiar and unexpected. *Phweet, Phweet, Phweet, Phweet, Phweeeeeeee!*

Is that Margret back with some food? Heinz looked around but didn't see her anywhere. There it was again. *Phweet, Phweet, Phweet, Phweet, Phweeeeeeee!*

Right front, Sgt Leopold (Poldi) Lister, London, England, of the 12th A Group Publicity and Psychological Warfare (PPW) at receivers in Rue Bressere Lux, Luxembourg. When Poldi joined the British army, he changed his name from Lichtenstern to Lister.

He turned in every direction to find the source of the whistle. There was a British soldier, and the whistling was coming from . . .

"Poldi!" Heinz yelled. It was his brother. He ran to embrace him. "How did you find me?"

"Heinz, I'm in British Intelligence. We know things." He smiled. "Actually, I've been monitoring the lists of survivors for weeks," Poldi said. "I really didn't hold out too much hope, but then, there were your names! 'Dutch survivors in Theresienstadt.' I got here as fast as I could. Where are Margret and the children? Aren't they here with you?"

"They've gone to look for some food," Heinz answered. With their arms around one another's shoulders, the two brothers returned to the baggage cart where Heinz and Margret had agreed to meet.

It was only a moment before Heinz spotted Margret with the children. He could see that Tutti and Robbie were bickering and occasionally pushing one another. Heinz figured they hadn't found anything to eat and were hungry. Margret walked ahead of the children with her head down, as if too weary to reprimand them. It took her a moment to realize that Heinz was not alone, and another minute to realize who the other man was. She stared in disbelief.

"Poldi?" she said.

"It's *me!*" He opened his arms to give her a huge hug.

The children stood close by. They didn't recognize their uncle. Poldi had moved to London in 1939, when Tutti was four and Robbie was one. It was as if they were meeting him for the first time. They said hello politely, but for them the best thing about the reunion was how genuinely happy Mammi and Pappi were.

When Margret suggested they find some food, everyone agreed. Poldi lifted Robbie onto his shoulders as they walked away from the station.

Heinz held Tutti's hand and looked at his daughter, beaming. "I saw you arguing with Robbie before," he said. "You mustn't fight. He's your *brother!*"

And into that word, he put all his joy at being with his own brother once again.

46

Knocking on Doors

July–August 1945

❧

Poldi accompanied Heinz in his search for a place to live. They walked through the city looking for apartments for rent and knocked on many doors. But each time, they were met with disappointment.

"Hello, is your apartment still available?" Heinz asked the first landlord, using his best Dutch.

"You are German, no?" the man replied upon hearing his accent.

"Yes, but I'm Jewish. I—" started Heinz.

"The room is not available to Germans!" interrupted the man, and he shut the door.

Other people wouldn't rent to him because he was Jewish. Still others wanted more than he could afford.

Heinz knew he would have a job, but he didn't have it yet. Lissauer, his old boss and owner of Oxyde, had escaped to Brazil and would want work in the Amsterdam office to resume, especially given that Europe would be rebuilding everything from sewers to bridges. Heinz would be able to earn money. But right now, he needed a place to live, someplace safe and inexpensive.

Finally, he had a break. Mrs. Muller was a kind-faced woman. When Heinz spoke, she wasn't upset by his accent.

He told her he was Jewish, and her reaction was one of compassion, rather than prejudice. She sighed and simply said, "The past few years have been hard."

Heinz thought she was about his mother's age. She said that she was born in Germany but had been living in Amsterdam since she was a child. Her husband had died of pneumonia last winter, and she was renting out one room in her apartment to make ends meet. When Heinz explained his situation, she agreed to rent to him. The room was small, but it would accommodate everyone.

On their way back to rejoin Margret and the children, Heinz couldn't stop worrying about his parents back in Sittard. He was in Amsterdam with a place to live, but his parents were still in that displaced persons camp. "Poldi, I've been thinking about our parents. You need to go to Sittard and see if you can get them out of there."

"I was just thinking the same thing. I'll leave first thing tomorrow."

"Good. Do whatever you can. I can't stand the thought of their being there one more minute! They need to come home."

The family lived in the rented room for a little over a month. Meanwhile, Heinz focused his energy on making a living again. He also looked for an apartment for his parents. He wanted them to have a place to call their own when they returned. And he didn't want them to face the same sting of anti-Semitism that he had encountered before finding Mrs. Muller.

By August, Heinz had Oxyde up and running. Now that he had a steady paycheck, he decided to talk to Adriaan Vos once more about recovering his family's belongings.

One morning before work, he walked the few kilometers to his old neighborhood. There was the building—badly in need of repair. He wondered who lived there now. It had been an NSB man in the days when Heinz had worked next door. He recalled his small aggression—leaving the cigarette butts on the man's stoop. But that was in the past. Now he had to think about the future.

When Vos answered Heinz's knock, he looked surprised. Heinz had barely managed to say hello before Vos interrupted him. "Nobody thought you would be back," he said flatly. "We were promised that no Jews would return. All of your things are gone." Then he shut the door and locked it.

Heinz stood staring at the closed door, hardly able to believe what had happened. Then the shock gave way to anger. He had thought this man was a friend! But he was nothing but a Nazi sympathizer.

Heinz knew he would never see justice.

47

Gifts

Late August 1945

❧

One day, as the family was getting ready to move into their new apartment, Tutti woke up with a runny nose and a sore throat. She was tired and coughing and fighting a fever. Mammi placed her hand on Tutti's forehead and said she was warm. "Tutti, I have to go out, but I'll be back as soon as I can. Mrs. Muller will stay here with you. Please try to nap."

"Okay, Mammi," said Tutti. She tried to sleep but couldn't get comfortable. Mrs. Muller brought her a cup of tea and a few small biscuits. "Drink the tea, Tutti. It'll help you feel better," she said, seating herself on the end of Tutti's bed.

The tea soothed her scratchy throat. She sat up with Popje beside her and told Mrs. Muller how Pappi had surprised her with Popje as a birthday present. She didn't say anything about the money that had been hidden inside the doll, but she realized she had no idea if it was still there. She wondered if Pappi had used it.

As she was thinking, Mrs. Muller interrupted her thoughts. "I have a present for you, too."

"You do?" asked Tutti in surprise.

"Yes. I hope you like it." From her apron pocket, Mrs. Muller pulled out a necklace and held it up for Tutti to see.

"*Dank u!* It's beautiful!" Tutti was delighted and she smiled for the first time all day. She took the shiny chain from Mrs. Muller and tried to fasten it around her neck.

"Let me help," said the elderly woman. "Oh, it looks lovely on you. I'm glad. Now close your eyes and rest."

❧   ❧   ❧

Tutti woke up when her mother kissed her forehead. "How are you feeling, Tuttchen?" Mammi asked, seating herself on the bed beside Tutti. "You're still a little warm."

"Mammi, look what Mrs. Muller gave me!" Tutti held out the pendant for her mother to see.

Mammi stared. Her eyes grew big, but she didn't smile.

"Don't you like it, Mammi? I think it's pretty."

After several seconds, Mammi answered her. "Tutti, it certainly is, but you can't keep it. We have to give it back to Mrs. Muller."

"Margret, I gave it to her. I really don't need it. It's been sitting in a drawer gathering dust for years," insisted Mrs. Muller.

"I want to keep it, Mammi. Can't I?" asked Tutti.

"No, I'm afraid not. Mrs. Muller, I know you meant well. However, my daughter cannot wear this necklace. Tutti, do you know what that is?"

"It's a 'T' for Tutti!" she answered.

"No, Tuttchen, it's a cross," explained Mammi.

"I think it looks like a 'T,'" said Tutti. She didn't want to argue with Mammi, but she wanted to keep the present.

"Tutti, I'm sorry. After everything we went through—" Mammi stopped talking and stood up abruptly. Then she added more gently, "We are Jewish, and Jews don't wear crosses. Please take it off now and give it back to Mrs. Muller."

With tears in her eyes, Tutti took off her shiny new necklace and handed it back.

❧   ❧   ❧

When Heinz came home from work that evening, he looked in on Tutti. "Are you feeling better?" he asked.

"Mammi says my temperature is all back to normal," she said. "But I'm still a little tired."

"Of course. That's to be expected, Tuttchen," he said, pulling a colorful bunch of flowers from behind his back and placing the vase on his daughter's bedside table.

Tutti sat up in bed to admire the bouquet. "Ooh, they're beautiful, Pappi—thank you!"

"You're welcome," he said, smiling. "Mammi told me about the necklace you had to return to Mrs. Muller today. And while I absolutely agree with Mammi, I thought perhaps these flowers might cheer you up."

Tutti leaned over to inhale their scent. "I'd forgotten how much I missed this smell, Pappi," she said.

"We've missed out on quite a lot for too long, haven't we?"

"Yes," said Tutti.

"And I don't think I've mentioned this to you before . . . which was wrong of me—I shouldn't have waited."

"What's that, Pappi?"

Heinz cleared his throat before continuing. "I just want you to know, Tuttchen, how courageous I think you *were* . . . and *are*. And how pleased I am about how loving you are with your brother—*most* of the time." With that, they both laughed. "No, seriously, Tutti, I couldn't be more proud of you. We're going to be all right—*all* of us. And that includes Popje here," he said, gently patting the doll's head as Tutti scooched back down on her pillows. "She's been a real lifesaver." Pappi pulled the blankets up and tucked Tutti in with a wink and a kiss good night.

"Rest well now," Pappi said.

Tutti understood that her father was sharing something important with her, and that made her feel very grown up. "*Gute Nacht,* Pappi," she said. "I love you."

"You too, Tuttchen, with all my heart."

With Popje safe in her arms, Tutti happily drifted off to sleep—the most peaceful sleep she'd had in a very long time.

❧

dank u (dahngk oo): thank you (Dutch)

48

Rebuilding

Fall 1945

❧

That fall, Egbert de Jong came to see Heinz in his office at Oxyde. He brought with him an envelope full of cash, and it lay on the desk between the two men as they talked. It was most of the money that Heinz had given Egbert for safe-keeping and for buying passports. Now Egbert wanted to return what was left and to account for every guilder that he had spent.

"Egbert, I don't want the money. And you didn't need to keep track of the cash like this. I trust you."

"I know you trust me. But you said it wasn't just *your* money. Other people contributed, as well. I didn't want anyone coming to me and saying I had handled the funds improperly."

"I suppose you're right. But please keep what's left. You took tremendous risks." Heinz pushed the envelope toward Egbert.

"No, Heinz, I'm not the one who spent a year and a half in Nazi camps. You keep it." Egbert slid the envelope back.

"I should return it to the people who contributed, Egbert."

"Heinz, you know as well as I do that you can't. Most of them didn't make it."

Heinz knew his friend was right. They sat in silence, each remembering those who were murdered by the Nazis simply because they were Jewish.

Egbert spoke first. "And the few who did come home, well, you use that money to restore Oxyde to the vibrant company it used to be and give them jobs. Steady employment is better than a handful of guilders."

❧ ❧ ❧

Heinz and Margret did everything in their power to get life back to normal. Heinz knew they were very fortunate. They had survived the war and, for the most part, they had trusted the right people.

Of Oxyde's one hundred employees, only about ten survived.

Heinz found himself at the top. As director, he went to work early every day. Europe was a shambles and everyone was trying to rebuild. Raw materials were in high demand. Heinz was busily engaged, buying and selling metal from around the world, including scrap from Rommel's abandoned German tanks in the African desert.

By the time Egbert had come to see him, Heinz had already moved his family into an apartment on Deurloostraat. This was much better than rooming with Mrs. Muller. The children had their own bedrooms, there was a proper kitchen and living room, and there was a full bathroom, as well.

As for Tutti and Robbie, they adapted relatively quickly, made friends with other children in the neighborhood, and returned to school. Having missed three years of education meant that they had a lot of work to do. Thankfully, their teachers were patient and they tried to be understanding when the two of them became frustrated now and again.

One of Heinz's coworkers at Oxyde tutored Tutti, and as she progressed, she helped Robbie with his studies. Margret and Heinz put an end to Robbie's habit of stealing—something he had picked up in the camps—and succeeded in teaching him right from wrong.

This was their new life. The children accepted it more readily than Heinz and Margret, because for them, there were lasting effects.

For the rest of Margret's life, goodbyes always brought her to tears. And Heinz vowed to never be vulnerable again. He dedicated his life to protecting his family.

49

Remember

Summer 1946

❧

One day, after walking in the park with Okkie and Muttchen, Tutti and Robbie returned home to find their mother sitting in the dining room with photos spread out over the table. They had recently moved back to De Lairessestraat, the same street they had been living on when the Germans invaded the Netherlands. Before the war, they had lived at number 4 on the garden level, and now they were at number 6 on the fourth floor. Okkie and Muttchen were living just a few blocks away on Valeriusstraat, between their son's home and the Vondelpark. Margret had been very busy for the past several weeks, once again unpacking boxes and setting up the house to make it a comfortable place for them all to live. She hoped this would be their last move.

"What are you doing, Mammi?" asked Robbie.

"I'm looking through all of these old photographs. Come see," she answered.

The children sat at the table with her and passed the photos back and forth.

"Mammi, why haven't we seen these pictures before?"

"We didn't have them for a long time. I just got them back today," she answered. "This morning, I had a visitor. Do you remember your nanny, Juffie?"

Flo and Louis Spier   Flo Spier in her winter garden

Margret (left) with her brother, Bobby, and sister, Gerta

"No," answered Robbie.

"A little," answered Tutti.

"She worked for us when the war started. I had forgotten that I'd given her these for safekeeping. She told me she'd forgotten too, but while sorting her belongings, she found them. So she called Pappi's office to find out if we'd, if we'd—"

"If we'd survived the war, Mammi?" Tutti finished her mother's sentence for her.

"Yes, Tutti. And then they told her where we lived and she rushed right over."

"Mammi, is this a picture of Oma Flo?" asked Robbie.

"Yes, that's your grandmother. She loved to tend to the cacti in her winter garden. My mother was so full of life."

"Mammi, I miss Oma Flo," said Tutti.

"So do I, Tuttchen. I miss her very much." Her eyes grew wet with tears.

"Who are these children, Mammi?" asked Tutti.

"This is your uncle Bobby, my sister Gerta, and me." Her voice cracked.

"I'm sorry! I didn't mean to make you sad!" Tutti quickly found a handkerchief and handed it to her mother.

"It's okay, Tuttchen. You didn't make me sad. The war did. Poor Bobby," she said, dabbing her eyes. "We lost him, too."

"Should we put the photos away, Mammi?" asked Tutti.

"Not yet. I like seeing them."

"Is this Opa Louis?" asked Robbie.

"Yes. Isn't he handsome? He was so composed and sweet and proper."

"I miss Opa Louis, too," said Robbie.

"We all do." Mammi stared at the pictures.

Tutti searched through the photos for a picture that might change Mammi's mood. She pointed to her parents' wedding photo. They looked so young and hopeful then.

"Mammi, why are you still crying?" Tutti asked. "This is a picture from a happy day!"

"There are a lot of feelings in these photographs, Tutti."

When Heinz came home, he joined his family at the table. "Margret, where did you get these?" he asked. He picked up one picture after another. Tutti noticed his eyes were tearing with emotion.

"Juffrouw Catharina brought them today."

"I had forgotten. They're so precious—our entire past. Our whole life before the war," said Pappi.

"We have been through so much and have lost too many people we loved," said Mammi.

"Like Uncle Bobby and Aunt Tineke," said Tutti.

"And Oma Flo and Opa Louis," said Robbie.

"Yes. And we went through some very bad times being cold and hungry and scared," said Pappi.

"These photo albums are full of special memories," said Mammi. "They are pictures from before the war—of our family and friends and of places where we enjoyed life. I know you will never forget the terrible things we've been through, *Kinder*, but I want you to recall the good times, as well."

Tenderly, she held her children's hands. "And I'd like you to always try to *do* good in the world—by speaking up when you see evil, and by behaving in a way that you know is right, no matter what others may be doing."

Pappi stood behind the children with his hands on their shoulders and bent to kiss their heads.

"Will you remember to do these things?" Mammi asked.

Robbie nodded his head and gave his mother a hug.

"I will," said Tutti. "I promise."

Tutti with Popje, speaking at the Connecticut State House, 2016

Words of Wisdom from Tutti

2016

I have kept Popje safe all this time. At first, I put her on display in my room and, when I got older, I put her away in my closet. Now I bring her with me when I go to schools to tell students my story of living through the Holocaust.

When I introduce Popje to children, I hope they will understand what she means to me and what we went through together. I want her to be a symbol for them—to remind them to be nice to each other. Don't judge. Don't bully. Help when you can. We are all human, no matter what religion, race, age, or sexual orientation. It doesn't matter where you were born, if you are rich or poor, what you look like, or whether you are able-bodied or have physical or mental challenges—none of these things should separate you from other people.

When you see bad things happening in the world, step up and do something. Even if that thing is small. We all have to work to make this world better.

I hope you learned something from my story. It's a story of hope and perseverance. It's a story of courage and compassion and luck. Most of all, it's a story that reminds us that we must never forget what prejudice and hatred can lead to if we don't confront them together.

Author's Note

When my mother speaks to school groups about her experiences during the Holocaust, I watch the children. They are captivated. Often, they have tears in their eyes. Some have read *The Diary of a Young Girl* by Anne Frank. Others have read *Night* by Elie Wiesel. They are studying World War II and the Holocaust in school, but the woman who is standing in front of their class lived through it. The students listen quietly, without fidgeting. They are respectful and truly honored to have her as a guest speaker.

I wonder to myself how many more times she will do this. She is healthy and strong for her age, but how much longer will she be willing and able to tell her story? The students in these classes are among the last generation that will hear survivors or witnesses of the Holocaust.

The children ask many questions, and she answers them all carefully and thoughtfully. They ask about the small details: what were the mattresses made of? They ask spiritual questions: did her faith help her through? And they ask deeper questions: what did she miss the most?

I believe the most important question is this: What does "never forget" mean? It is the reason that my mother continues to tell her story and teachers continue to invite her to come to their classrooms. Never forget. People say it when they talk about the Holocaust, and it can take on many meanings. Some say that it means we have to remember the victims. Some say we need to honor the survivors. And others say we need to fight anti-Semitism. All of that is true.

For me, "never forget" means we need to learn from history. We need to understand that prejudice hurts: it injures the people who are discriminated against, and it damages the people who hold the biased views. Emphasizing differences between people and using those disparities to demean or intimidate others is insensitive and cruel. Instead, we need to notice our similarities as human beings and find ways to bridge the gaps that divide us in order to move forward toward positive human relations. "Never forget" reminds us that seven billion people need to find a way to live peacefully on this one small planet.

In 2007, at the age of seventy-two, my mother began speaking to school groups about her experiences. Since then, thousands of students have listened to her presentation. This book will ensure that her story is never forgotten.

❧   ❧   ❧

My mother, my uncle Robbie, my grandparents, and my mother's paternal grandparents survived the Holocaust. But my mother's uncle Bobby and her maternal grandparents, Flo and Louis, perished, murdered at Auschwitz. I never had the privilege of knowing them. Bobby's wife died in Mauthausen, less than two months before the camp was liberated.

From July 15, 1942, through September 13, 1944, 103 transports departed Westerbork for the East, carrying 14,502 children. The fates of Tutti's friends mentioned in this book are as follows: Ursula Heilbut was murdered at Auschwitz on October 21, 1944, when she was just nine years old; and Klaus Walbaum was killed at Auschwitz on October 6, 1944, at age eleven. Gaby Silten survived. At this writing, she lives in California. Ursula Levy and Gerd Aschenbrand also lived, but Michael Finkelstein perished.

Sadly, my grandparents' friend Max Ehrlich was murdered at Auschwitz, but his wife, Lotte, survived and settled in Amsterdam. She and Margret remained close for many years. Okkie's friend Dr. Ernst Keller survived and then resided in Vienna.

After the war, Egbert de Jong was accused of collaborating with the Germans. He was jailed for a couple of months while there was an investigation, but he was soon cleared. The de Jong and Lichtenstern families continued their friendship after the war, with the children referring to Egbert as Uncle Eg.

Another person from this story who was accused of collaboration was Leopold Oberländer. He and his wife, Lilli, survived Westerbork. Leopold was eventually cleared. Josef and Else Sax survived the war in hiding and lived in Amsterdam after the war.

While I have not yet found evidence that the sabotaging of Nazi Germany's metal resulted in any catastrophic failures of planes or U-boats, that doesn't mean that my grandfather and his colleagues-in-arms were *not* successful. They certainly slowed the war machine down, and I'd like to believe that their actions caused many problems for the Nazis. But whether or not *those* objectives were achieved, their work saved lives. Their daring determination was thus a singular act of defiance and resistance against annihilation and brutality and an immense humanitarian achievement.

The money in Popje's head was only one factor among many that saved members of my family. Numerous people gave them help, encouragement, and the things they needed to survive. Mr. Lissauer relocated my family from the German office to Amsterdam; and after the war, he gave my grandfather his job back. Friedrich von Oppenheim offered to smuggle them out of the country. The Klopfers risked their own lives by hiding them in their attic. Egbert de Jong and Jakob Jorysch obtained the Paraguayan passport for the family and helped them get out of Westerbork. The Nazi guard let my grandfather take vegetables to feed his family. Max Ehrlich lifted everyone's spirits the only way he knew how, with jokes. When the war was over, the Russian soldiers showed kindness with oranges and chocolate bars, while the American soldiers, Lloyd Miller and Stanley Greenberg*, befriended this small group of refugees. My great-uncle Poldi searched the lists of survivors and came as soon as possible to help his brother and parents get re-established. Mrs. Muller rented them a room when others would not.

Of course, there were also those people who took advantage of our family—people like Mr. Vos, for example, who sold off our family's possessions, assuming no one would come home to claim them.

Mostly, though, there were the bystanders who did nothing.

My mother, her little brother, Robbie, her parents, and her father's parents survived a terrible part of human history. Of the six million Jews who perished, more than one million were children. According to the International Institute for Holocaust Research at Yad Vashem, "children were considered non-productive and symbolized the continuation of Jewish existence," so "they were among the first victims who were sent to their deaths in order to ensure the total destruction of the Jewish people."**

Of the approximately 140,000 Jews living in the Netherlands at the time of the German invasion on May 10, 1940, more than 75 percent perished—mostly at Auschwitz and Sobibor. Twenty-five to thirty thousand went into hiding, and about two-thirds of them were able to survive. In all, the Germans deported 107,000 Jewish people from the Netherlands to Nazi camps, of whom only 5,200—or 5 percent—lived.

In the end, it wasn't one thing that saved Tutti's family. A combination of luck, the kindness of friends and strangers, the wisdom of planning ahead, and most of all, courage and perseverance made it possible for the Lichtensterns to survive the Holocaust.

*The name Stanley Greenberg is fictitious, as Tutti cannot recall his real name.
**http://www.yadvashem.org

The Lichtenstern Family Tree (2016)

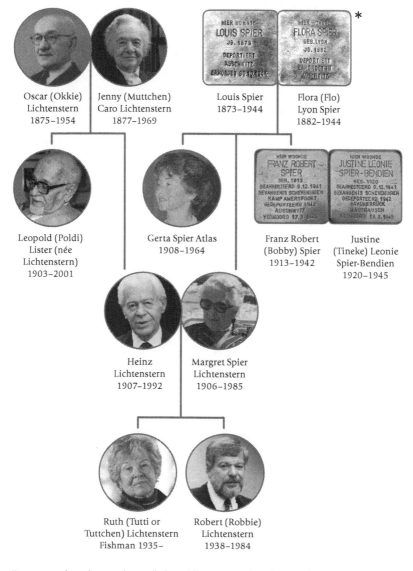

Oscar (Okkie) Lichtenstern 1875–1954

Jenny (Muttchen) Caro Lichtenstern 1877–1969

Louis Spier 1873–1944

Flora (Flo) Lyon Spier 1882–1944 *

Leopold (Poldi) Lister (née Lichtenstern) 1903–2001

Gerta Spier Atlas 1908–1964

Franz Robert (Bobby) Spier 1913–1942

Justine (Tineke) Leonie Spier-Bendien 1920–1945

Heinz Lichtenstern 1907–1992

Margret Spier Lichtenstern 1906–1985

Ruth (Tutti or Tuttchen) Lichtenstern Fishman 1935–

Robert (Robbie) Lichtenstern 1938–1984

*Learn more about these markers, called stumbling stones, at http://www.stolpersteine.eu/en/home/

Glossary

Unless stated otherwise, the words in this glossary are German. In German, the first letter of a common noun is capitalized.

Foreign Word	English Translation
Abwehr (**ahp** • vehr)	German Military Intelligence
alles gut (**ahl** • luhs goot)	all's well
auf Wiedersehen (owf **vee** • dehr • zehn)	goodbye
ausgeschieden (**ows** • geh • **shee** • dehn)	withdrawn
Blauwe Theehuis (**blau** • uh **tay** • house)	Blue Teahouse (Dutch)
chutzpah (**khoots** • puh)	nerve (Yiddish)
dank u (**dahngk** oo)	thank you (Dutch)
een minuut (ayn mih • **noot**)	one minute (Dutch)
goedendag (**khoo** • duh • **dahkh**)	good day (Dutch)
Gott im Himmel (got ihm **him** • mehl)	God in heaven
guilders (**gil** • duhrs)	Dutch currency (English)
gute Nacht (**goo** • tuh nah<u>kht</u>)	good night
Gute Nacht. Schlaf gut, meine Kinder. (**goo** • tuh nah<u>kht</u>; shlahf **goot**, **mine** • uh **kihn** • dehr)	Good night. Sleep well, my children.
guten Morgen (**goo** • tuhn **mohr** • guhn)	good morning
guten Tag (**goo** • tuhn **tahk**)	good day

hallo (hah•**loh**)	hello (Dutch)
Herr (hehr)	Mr.
ja (yah)	yes (Dutch)
ja, alstublieft (yah, ahls•tew•**bleeft**)	yes, please (Dutch)
jawohl (yah•**vohl**)	yes
Jood (yote)	Jew (Dutch)
Juffie (**yoof**•ee)	A nickname meaning "Missy" (Dutch)
Kinder (**kihn**•dehr)	children
kinderen (**kihn**•duh•ruhn)	children (Dutch)
Mädchen (**mayt**•chehn)	girl
manneke (**mah**•neh•kuh)	little man (Dutch)
mein kleines Mädchen (mine **kline**•ehs **mayt**•chehn)	my little girl
Muttchen (**muhtch**•ehn)	Granny
nein (nine)	no
Okkie (**aw**•kee)	a nickname for Oscar
Oma (**oh**•mah)	grandmother
Opa (**oh**•pah)	grandfather
politie (poh•**leet**•see)	police (Dutch)
popje (**pop**•yah)	dolly (Dutch)
prikkeldraad soep (**prih**•kehl•**draht** soop)	barbed wire soup (Dutch)
schlaf gut (shlahf **goot**)	sleep well
schnell (shnehl)	quickly
sedni (**sehd**•nyih)	sit down (Czech)

Sicherheitspolizei (**zikh**•uhr•hites•**poh**•leet•**tzahy**)	Security Police
stroopwafel (**strohp**•wah•fuhl)	a caramel-filled waffle (Dutch)
Theresienstadt (teh•**ray**•zee•uhn•**shtaht**)	A fortress in German-controlled Czechoslovakia used by the Nazis as a transit/ghetto-labor camp (see Historical Notes)
Tutti (**too**•tee)	Ruth Lichtenstern's nickname
Tuttchen (**tuhtch**•ehn)	An endearing nickname for Tutti
um Gottes Willen (oom **gawt**•ehs **vill**•uhn)	for God's sake
vorsichtig (**fohr**•zish•tish)	careful
Was ist los? (**vahs** ist lohs)	What's wrong?

Historical Notes

Chapter 1

The **radio transcript** in this chapter can be found on the Dutch website Go2War2.NL; the English translation is excerpted from https://translate.google.com/translate?hl=en&sl=nl&u=http://www.go2war2.nl/print.asp%3Fartikelid%3D2366&prev=search.

A translation of the **Queen's proclamation** (paraphrased in this chapter) is available at https://www.newspapers.com/clip/5832151/queen_wilhelminas_proclamationspeech/.

Chapter 2

The role of topography and geography in the fate of the Jews in the Netherlands is discussed by Linda Wolf in "Survival and Resistance: The Netherlands under Nazi Occupation," http://faculty.webster.edu/woolflm/netherlands.html.

Chapter 3

Metal traders buy and sell metals for businesses and governments. They make money themselves by charging a commission.

Aryan is defined by Nazi ideology as a white person of non-Semitic descent. The Nazis considered Aryans to be racially superior to non-Aryans.

Chapter 4

As Egbert warned Heinz in March 1941, the Nazis announced that fall that all financial assets held by Jews had to be deposited into one particular holding company—the Lipmann Rosenthal Bank (also known as LIRO)—the first step in seizing those assets for themselves.

130,000 guilders in 1941 is equivalent to more than $500,000 US dollars in 2017.

Chapter 6
The lullaby *"Weißt du, wieviel Sternlein stehen"* was written by J. Wilhelm Hey in the 1830s. The translation in the chapter is by John H. W. Dulcken; see the website hymntime.com at http://www.hymntime.com/tch/htm/d/y/k/dykhmstr.htm.

Chapter 8
Gestapo is short for Geheimstaatspolizei, or Secret State Police. The Gestapo was the official secret police force of Nazi Germany and German-occupied Europe.

Chapter 9
The Jewish Councils were created by the Nazis during the war to ensure that their orders were carried out in the ghettos, but the councils also tried to provide Jews living in the ghetto with some basic services. Heinz was on the less powerful Advisory Committee for non-Dutch Jews. For more about the councils and their "impossible moral dilemmas," see the U.S. Holocaust Memorial Museum website at https://www.ushmm.org/wlc/en/article.php?ModuleId=10005265.

The SS (short for Schutzstaffel, or Protection Squadron) was an extremely powerful Nazi paramilitary force that carried out the Nazis' campaign to eradicate the Jews.

Chapter 10
On October 10, 1996, Yad Vashem recognized **Baron Friedrich von Oppenheim** as Righteous Among the Nations: http://db.yadvashem.org/righteous/family. html?language=en&itemId=4043015

Untersturmführer was a rank in the SS.

Chapter 14
The Lichtensterns joined between 25,000 and 30,000 of their fellow Jews living in **hiding** in the Netherlands. Among them were the Franks—including fourteen-year-old Anne—who had also fled Germany to Amsterdam in the early 1930s, only to become trapped when the Germans invaded the Netherlands in May 1940.

Chapter 16
The Jewish Theater (Joodsche Schouwburg) was originally called the Dutch Theater (Hollandsche Schouwburg). The name was changed in 1941 after the Nazis decreed that the theater was for Jewish performers and Jewish audiences only. Later, the Nazis used it as a gathering place before deportations. Today it is a memorial site and a museum.

Chapter 19
The Sicherheitsdienst (also known as the SD) was the security and information service of the SS.

Chapter 20
Aryanization refers to the forced expulsion of non-Aryans, mainly Jews, from businesses. It entailed the transfer of Jewish property into Aryan possession.

The NSB (short for Nationaal-Socialistische Beweging) was the Dutch political party that sympathized with and supported the Nazis.

The **black market** was a system for illegally buying and selling goods.

Heil Hitler was a greeting used by Nazis, accompanied by a straight-armed salute. It was mandatory for civilians to address high-ranking military officers this way.

A U-boat, short for the German *Unterseeboot*, is a submarine.

Chapter 21

While the **Oxyde Jews,** as they had come to be called by the Germans, worked away on their plans, the Nazis were also unraveling their promises to let the metal buyers remain in Amsterdam. Hitler had given Adolf Eichmann a job—to clear occupied Europe of every Jew once and for all. But Albert Speer, Hitler's minister of armaments and munitions, needed metal. These two men had opposing goals. Speer needed the Oxyde Jews to continue working, while Eichmann, knowing they were among the last free Jews in the Netherlands, wanted them out.

In January 1944, while the captain in charge of metal acquisition for the Armaments Division was on vacation, an order for the arrest of the Oxyde Jews was drawn up. Adolf Eichmann's office insisted that these last Jewish families be taken to Westerbork and then East. Officials in the Armaments Division and Eichmann's office sent memos back and forth, arguing about what to do. In the end, an arrest order was issued with a compromise: once arrested, the Oxyde Jews would be given preferred housing within the camps and ultimately be sent to Theresienstadt.

On February 10, 1944, Wilhelm Zoepf, one of the top SS officers in charge of the deportation of Jews from the Netherlands, ordered the arrest of Josef Sax, Leopold Oberländer, and Heinz Lichtenstern, along with their families.

Euterpestraat was the street where the Gestapo headquarters was located in Amsterdam.

Chapter 22
Theresienstadt was a transit/ghetto-labor camp for three and a half years, between November 24, 1941 and May 9, 1945.

"In Nazi propaganda, Theresienstadt was cynically described as a 'spa town' where elderly German Jews could 'retire' in safety. The deportations to Theresienstadt were, however, part of the Nazi strategy of deception. The ghetto was in reality a collection center for deportations to ghettos and killing centers in Nazi-occupied eastern Europe."
—US Holocaust Memorial Museum: https://www.ushmm. org/wlc/en/article.php?ModuleId=10005424

Chapter 25
Amsterdam Centraal is the main train station in Amsterdam.

Chapter 29
There were 2,074 people on Transport VII from Westerbork to Theresienstadt on September 4, 1944.

Max Ehrlich was a famous comedian and film star. He was sent to Westerbork at the beginning of 1943 and applied to Gemmeker for permission to establish a theater group. Gemmeker agreed, hoping that performances would distract prisoners, impress foreign visitors, and entertain the camp staff. See the website Music and the Holocaust at http://holocaustmusic.ort.org/places/camps/western-europe/westerbork/.

The jokes in the text are paraphrased from *Heulen und Zähneklappern,* by Max Ehrlich and Paul Morgan (1927).

Chapter 31
Theresienstadt: Four months after Tutti's grandparents arrived, they saw one area that looked better cared for than the rest, with new paint and clean windows. The section had been specially prepared by the Nazis for a scheduled visit by the International Red Cross which, in June 1944, came to Theresienstadt to investigate claims that the Nazis were mistreating the Jews.

The Nazis made sure that the bakery and butcher shop had windows full of delicious foods, and allowed only the healthiest-looking people to be outside. Hitler even arranged for professional filmmakers to record the "beautiful town" and the "happy Jews" living there. The guards, with their guns, had stood just out of reach of the cameras. As part of this "elaborate hoax, the Germans intensified deportations from the ghetto shortly before the [Red Cross] visit, and the ghetto itself was 'beautified.' Gardens were planted, houses painted, and barracks renovated. The Nazis staged social and cultural events for the visiting dignitaries. Once the visit was over, the Germans resumed deportations from Theresienstadt, which did not end until October 1944. . . . Of the approximately 140,000 Jews transferred to Theresienstadt, nearly 90,000 were deported to points further east and almost certain death." (US Holocaust Memorial Museum)

Chapter 35
Theresienstadt was extremely overcrowded. The barracks were infested with fleas, lice, and bedbugs, which created outbreaks of all sorts of illnesses, such as typhus, scarlet fever, and dysentery. About 33,000 people died in Theresienstadt due to these terrible living conditions. Tutti and Robbie's mother knew how important hygiene was to health and was determined to keep her children as safe as humanly possible.

Chapter 38
The main **Allied powers**—the United States, Great Britain, China, and the Soviet Union—were the countries that fought the Axis powers—Germany, Italy, and Japan.

Chapter 42
G.I. is a nickname for a soldier of the United States Army or Air Force.

Chapter 43
Repatriation is the process by which someone is sent back to the country of his or her birth or citizenship.

Displaced persons, or DPs, are people who are forced to leave their homes because of war, persecution, or natural disaster.

Chapter 44
The Nazis murdered Jews, Gypsies, homosexuals, and others through gassing, hanging, shooting, starvation, disease, and death marches. At one point, up to 6,000 Jews were gassed each day at Auschwitz with Zyklon B, a chemical originally developed to kill insects.

Chapter 46
The story of **Adriaan Vos,** the neighbor who sold off the family's possessions, is true, but his name has been changed.

Chapter 48
Erwin Johannes Eugen **Rommel** was a German field marshal who led the German and Italian forces in North Africa during World War II.

Chapter 49
Franz Robert Spier, Margret's brother, died at Auschwitz on August 17, 1942. He was twenty-nine years old. His wife, Justine (Tineke) Leonie Bendien, died at Mauthausen on March 19, 1945. She was twenty-four years old. They were first sent to a prison in Scheveningen, after having being caught while trying to escape from the Netherlands. Bobby, Tineke, and two of their friends wrote their names on a wall in the prison, which was nicknamed the "Orange Hotel." To learn more about their attempted escape, read *House of Memories: Uncovering the Past of a Dutch Jewish Family* (Hilversum, 2016), by Arnoud-Jan Bijsterveld.

Acknowledgements

I never could have written *Tutti's Promise* alone. Heartfelt thanks to the following people:

Katharine Britton, Joni Cole, Amanda Lynch D'Agostino, Kim Gifford, Diana Goetsch, Barbara Krasner, and workshop participants who helped me craft;

Staff at the Amsterdam City Archives, Beit Theresienstadt, Herinneringscentrum Kamp Westerbork, International Tracing Service, Jewish Historical Museum of Amsterdam, Jewish Museum in Prague, National Archives of the Netherlands, NIOD (including Erik Schumacher), NRW State Archive, Patton Museum, Terezín Memorial Ghetto, United States Holocaust Memorial Museum, and Yad Vashem;

Relatives of people featured in *Tutti's Promise:* Ger van den Berg, Alan Ehrlich, Jackie Gish, Joke van Krieken, Chaz Lichtenstern, Peter Lister, Franklin Oberländer, Christopher von Oppenheim, Jopie Pasman-de Jong, Gisela von Sanden, Marjan Sax, Nicky Wernick, as well as Edith Karfiol-Jorysch and Henny van den Berg, who passed too soon;

Survivors Ellen van Creveld, Frank Salz, Gabriele Silten, Judy Straus, and Hermine Weinreb Milgram, who shared their Holocaust experiences;

Brett Sigurdson of Champlain College and the League of Vermont Writers, who gave an invaluable critique;

Gunter Edler and Klaus and Ulrike Kruener, who provided background stories;

Crossroads Academy Middle School, Carolina Dahlqvist, Tina Jarrett, Leta Marks, Bozena Brzeczek Masters, and Trevor Siegel, who read early drafts;

Residents of Tutti's many addresses in Amsterdam; and Caroline Faber-van Hattem, who provided an Amsterdam home base;

Cheerleaders Nancy Brennan, Lori Lyth-Frantz, and Jim Rice;

Avinoam Patt from the University of Hartford, and the Holocaust Educator Award Committee at the Maurice Greenberg Center for Judaic Studies;

My amazing publisher, Margie Blumberg, and her wonderful team: Jim Catler (who in 1975, at age sixteen, interviewed Tutti as a volunteer for the Greater Hartford Jewish Historical Society), editor Anne Himmelfarb, and the designers at PageWave Graphics; and Dodge-Chrome, Inc., for the photographic restorations;

Special thanks to . . .

Arnoud-Jan Bijsterveld of Tilburg University and Myriam Daru, for extraordinary research assistance and guidance;

My husband, Dave, who put up with my obsession, listened to numerous drafts, and corrected my grammar;

And especially my mother, Tutti, the inspiration for it all.

Photo and Document Credits

All images are from the author's private collection unless otherwise noted.

Map: Courtesy of USMA Department of History

Prologue: Lena Stein

Ch. 4: From the private collection of Johanna Margaretha Maria van Krieken

Ch. 6: Star • United States Holocaust Memorial Museum, gift of Evelyn Levy Paswell. Used by permission from the USHMM. Collection 2012.487.2

Ch. 9: Jewish Council guide • Jewish Historical Museum, Amsterdam

Ch. 10: From the private collection of the von Oppenheim family

Ch. 14: From the private collection of Annette Heldt

Ch. 16: Image Bank WW2 – NIOD

Ch. 17: Main street • Herinneringscentrum Kamp Westerbork, Netherlands

Ch. 19: NIOD Amsterdam, collection 250i (transit camp Westerbork), inventory number 152 and used by permission of all living persons on the document

Ch. 21: Arrest order • Yad Vashem, Archival Signature: TR.3/610

Ch. 22: NIOD Amsterdam, archive 250i, inventory number 319 with permission of all living persons

Ch. 24: Do 788, Schrift metal, Schwarz, F. Herinneringscentrum Kamp Westerbork, Netherlands

Ch. 29: NIOD Amsterdam, archive 250i, inventory number 325

Ch. 32: From the personal collection of R. Gabriele S. Silten

Ch. 33: Jewish Museum in Prague, Terezín Collection, Box 19, Inventory no. 145, Daily bulletin of the Jewish self-administration no. 47, September 24th 1944.

Ch. 35: Helga Weissová, Zeichne, was Du siehst / Draw what you see, Zeichnungen eines Kindes aus Theresienstadt / Terezín, Hg. von Niedersächsischer Verein zur Förderung von Theresienstadt / Terezín e. V., © Wallstein Verlag, Göttingen 1998.

Ch. 36: National Archives in Prague, Occupation Prison and Penitentiary Files, List of deported people, Transport EV 28.10.1944 from Terezín to Auschwitz, page 644.

Ch. 37: Helga Weissová, Zeichne, was Du siehst / Draw what you see, Zeichnungen eines Kindes aus Theresienstadt / Terezín, Hg. von Niedersächsischer Verein zur Förderung von Theresienstadt / Terezín e. V., © Wallstein Verlag, Göttingen 1998.

Ch. 40: Yad Vashem Photo Archive, Jerusalem, Item ID: 73447; Archival Signature: 3174/62, Nezmany

Ch. 45: Heslop, J. Malan. Courtesy, L. Tom Perry Special Collections, Harold B. Lee Library, Brigham Young University, Provo, Utah.

Words of Wisdom from Tutti: Kathy Fishman

About the Author: David Smith

For Flo, Louis, Bobby, and Tineke.
You are not forgotten.

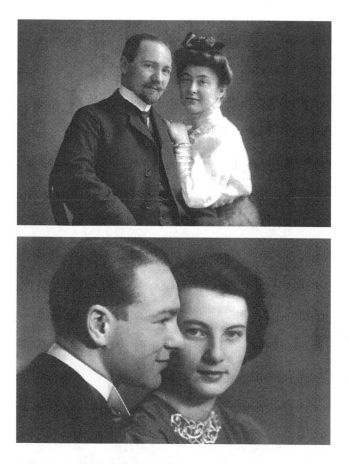

Top: Louis and Flora Spier (Tutti's maternal grandparents)
in 1905, the year they were married
Bottom: Franz Robert Spier (Tutti's uncle) and his wife,
Justine Leonie Spier-Bendien, on their wedding day,
January 6, 1940

About the Author

K. Heidi Fishman grew up in West Hartford, Connecticut. After graduating from Williams College, she received her MA and EdD in Counseling Psychology from Western Michigan University. She specialized in working with people with eating disorders and histories of trauma at Dartmouth College and, later, in private practice. In 2015, Heidi won the Joseph Zola Memorial Holocaust Educator Award from the Maurice Greenberg Center for Judaic Studies at the University of Hartford for the book proposal for *Tutti's Promise*. A mother of four, Heidi lives in Vermont with her husband and a feisty border terrier and occasionally sees her busy teenagers. Photographs, documents, research links, discussion questions, and Tutti's video testimony can be found at www.kheidifishman.com.

Made in the USA
Middletown, DE
25 June 2019